Praise for
CORRUPTED
Alpha's Claim, Book Five

"Prepare to fall in love with the villain. To obsess over every interaction, and to read the book from cover to cover, over and over again!" –NYT bestselling author, Anna Zaires

"Better than a dark lover running their thumb across your bottom lip. Get on your knees and read." - USA TODAY bestselling author, Myra Danvers

"Unconventional, passionate, thrilling! You'll be hooked from the first page!" –USA TODAY bestselling author, Alta Hensley

"A twisted and tantalizingly sensual treat that I devoured in one day!" –USA TODAY bestselling author, Zoe Blake

CORRUPTED

ALPHA'S CLAIM, BOOK FIVE

ADDISON CAIN

©2021 by Addison Cain
All rights reserved.

No part of the book may be reproduced or transmitted in any form or by any means, electronic or mechanical, including photocopying, recording, or by any information storage and retrieval system, without permission in writing from the author.

This is a work of fiction. Names, characters, businesses, places, events and incidents are either the products of the author's imagination or used in a fictitious manner. Any resemblance to actual persons, living or dead, or actual events is purely coincidental.

Illustrations by Zakuga
Cover art by Raven Designs
Photography by Wander Aguiar

For my darling husband. I appreciate everything you do.

And for Sharlene, who is a saint for putting up with my sometimes wild schedule.

1

BERNARD DOME

Awakening to the most glorious feelings of delight, Brenya smiled, nestling closer to what made the world perfect and new. Warm and protected, surrounded in scent, everything was lovely .

Fingers tripped down her spine, a satiny purr moving through her.

Fulfillment, conquest. Triumphant emotions stronger than any she'd ever known brought a satisfied flush to her cheeks and made her hum.

Until she realized they weren't hers.

Sucking in air as if suddenly drowning, finding her body was not floating but actually in a great deal of discomfort, Brenya mentally flailed in the river of another person's emotions.

"Shhhhhh."

It hit her stronger, the alien sentiment. It swept her panic aside as if her own much weaker feelings were meaningless.

"Don't fight it."

A forceful psyche prevailed.

Jacques.

Finding herself back in his rooms, in his bed, naked, was shock enough to stop the heart. Realizing none of those wonderful feelings had been real, broke it.

This was not right. She was supposed to be free. She'd gotten out, flown a craft. Why was she not in Thólos repairing their Dome?

Someone was inside her skin, and though she held her fingers up before her face and found she could control them, the invasion was there all the same.

"Take a deep breath." Jacques' hand came to her chest. When she obeyed, he added, "Good, now take another."

Calm—he was inundating her body with manipulative calm.

Brenya's next blink led to warm drips marking her temples. Staring up in horror, she whispered, "What have you done to me?"

Leaning over, his golden hair loose and spilling around her face, Jacques smiled. Brushing his lips over her eyes, he kissed away her tears. "Made you mine, Brenya. You're mine completely now. My pair-bonded mate."

Estrous, the ship, bottles of water rolling over the floor… the Beta warning her not to open the door.

Hours of unbearable pain…

The memories were foggy with only flashes she might

piece together, but a thrusting body had been on top of her. Someone had saved her from the pit of hell. Or had they dragged her to it? "It was you...."

"I was only a few hours behind you." Some of the Alpha's triumph was replaced with dangerous resentment. "You would have never made it, you know. That vessel was no match for the speed of my ship. I have an army of Alphas conditioned to throw themselves to their deaths on my order. Not a single one even questioned a mission that drew them from the safety of the Dome. I would have invaded Thólos myself if I'd had to."

And some of those Alphas had watched what she was beginning to remember. Shame formed in the pit of her stomach at the flashes of soldiers clad in bio-suits guarding the cockpit door.

Another with unnaturally vibrant blue eyes licking his lips as she moaned her release.

Cold, Brenya tried to turn to her side to shiver against the mattress. Jacques allowed it, settling against her back to toy with her hair and continue his internal gloating.

"I sense your dissatisfaction." Amazed, he scoffed at the back of her head. "You mistakenly believe that I will hurt you. I can practically read your thoughts, naughty girl."

This was a nightmare beyond comprehension, Brenya whispering, "Don't."

"And now you're scared, worried, lost—internally reaching out for your mate to comfort your fears. As you should." He rewarded her by forgetting his anger and filling her with his joy. "I never want you to feel afraid of me."

His manipulation was so outright, she could hardly resist.

"You don't believe me," he spoke what he sensed, even daring to sound surprised.

How could she? Tears fell in earnest as the truth sank in. "You're going to kill George."

"No, *mon chou*." His denial was echoed with raw internal confirmation. "The Beta is meaningless at this point."

Daring to glance over her shoulder despite a shooting pain that followed, she gave him a pathetic "No?"

He kissed her red nose and smiled. "Don't cry. I don't want you to fear that there will be any retaliation for your recent... *hormonal behavior*. You were punished and are forgiven."

She was humiliated. She was tired. And she was guilty of much more than *hormonal behavior*. "What's going to happen to me?"

The arm around her middle tightened as Jacques pulled her flush to his body. "I'm going to make you feel better."

"I'm sore."

Husky, he chuckled. "I don't doubt it. In estrous you were a very greedy girl."

Estrous had been awful, and had left her wasted, body and soul. She never wanted to think about it again, any of it.

Jacques was not going to allow that.

"You were glorious through all of it, even when you refused to behave. It was the necessary choice to make, and had I not loved you so much, I never could have abided sharing... but it *was* exciting watching you take us both at once. Feeling another inside you next to me, hearing you come undone." Rubbing his thickening cock between the cheeks of her ass, he whispered, "I came harder than I ever have before... and Gods, so did you."

Jacques was against her back now, mirroring the motion. Brenya knew he'd planned his assault in such a way so she would have tactile memory of the Ambassador grunting at her ear.

There was no way to describe the sensations. Even allowing a moment of recollection sent an unwanted tingle and a small dribble of slick to gather at her slit. "It was wrong."

Tongue slipping out to tease the shell of her ear, Jacques teased, "Far from wrong. I know what's best for my rebellious, naughty Omega."

The Commodore rolled his hips as if to penetrate what was his.

Brenya angled away.

In answer to her unspoken rejection, the male caught her hip, purring, "Just as this will make you feel better," while thrusting slowly in.

Exhaling in an effort to handle the unusual discomfort of the stretch, Brenya found she had no will left to fight, that her body was weak, and that it did feel good no matter how much she wished it did not.

"That's right. I can make my defiant Omega sweet as cream." He took her breast in his grip, withdrawing his cock before easing deeper with the second controlled thrust. "Before you know it, you'll whisper how much you love me."

Closing her eyes, because she could not close her ears, Brenya grew limp.

"That's right."

Her nipple distended, peaking under a rolling pinch, and with little more than a few minutes of slow fucking, she already began to feel the early flutters of climax.

Soft and easy, the ripple of her muscles drew out a growing knot. The Alpha's groaned reaction fed her pleasure, even if the muscles that clenched around him were tender, even if her heart was not in it.

His was. His heart was completely taken with her.

When it was done and his knot tied her to him, Jacques traced his finger over the gash on her shoulder and let out a satisfied sigh. "Now that you are awake, I'm going to kiss every wound, wash every scratch. Don't be alarmed by what you see in the mirror. Claiming marks are supposed to scar. Like the rest of you, they are beautiful."

Absently, she reached up to touch her neck where she hurt the most. There was a bandage covering the place Brenya remembered a stranger's teeth taking hold. "What happened to the Ambassador?"

A warm palm flattened on her shoulder, wrapping aching flesh in reverent fingers. "Jules Havel is the righthand man to the terrorist who destroyed Thólos. That is who you kidnapped and thought to take there—*a real monster* who has murdered millions of people. If your stolen ship had made it as far as the southern continent, you would have started a war Bernard Dome cannot win. Everyone you know, your George included, would have died. Their regime is merciless."

That could not be true…

But it was true; she could feel the sincerity of such a statement. The knot shrank, and she turned to finally look at the man who had caught her in his trap, shamed her before his men, and shared her with a stranger.

The lingering marks of her attack still bruised his face. His arrogant playfulness was gone.

"Why did you let him…?" Why had he ordered his soldiers to set such a man free and offered her body to him. Jacques had encouraged the Beta to fuck her, to bite her, to join in his fun. Why?

"Hush, now, Brenya. You misunderstand." He kissed her quickly, cuddling the repulsed female. "Please listen to me when I tell you that everything, every choice I made, was in your best interest."

She didn't want his games or misdirection. She wanted answers. "What happened to the Ambassador?"

"Can you not tell?"

"No." Growing horror brought fresh tears, because there was something whispering in her mind. Something about that moment on that ship that Jacques had manipulated her into. "No."

"He won't be able to hurt you. Ever. The pair-bond will prevent it."

It was too much. There was too much inside her, too much to bear. "What did you do, Jacques?"

"I put a rabid dog on a leash."

2

"You are angry with me." Exuding reason, chest vibrating a sleepy, warm blanket of a purr, Jacques held another bite of fine cheese to Brenya's mouth, patient for her to accept food from his hand. "And you feel unwell."

Eyes distant, her thoughts somewhere else entirely, she parted her lips and took the offering onto her tongue.

Not a morsel had passed that chapped skin that he had not placed there, hand feeding his new mate delicious things, sips of cool water, and a few coerced swallows of rare vintage white wine. A new mate who appeared more unfocused and startled than a freshly born calf.

And just as shaky on her legs.

More comforting elation he poured within the empty cup of what made her Omega, drowning out lingering, trifling disgust and total terror by manipulating the link as if an expert already. Dwarfing her slumped shoulders with careful strokes of big, warm hands, he offered relaxation. Yet all he offered failed to produce the desired result.

His Brenya was implacable on a soul-deep level. A place even he had not yet found a way to touch with the captivation of their bond or his more practiced pleasantries.

Jacques changed tactics. In place of luxury, he offered sympathy. "I was cruel to you, wasn't I?"

An instant internal flicker, silent agreement followed by a sniff.

Despite his aggressive manipulation and constant, relentless pull on their link, honeyed eyes welled. A single tear fell on her next blink. And by the Gods, it cut him to the core. That tear *gutted him*, so much more than her small agreement.

A small voice replied, "You were cruel."

In contrast to his height and strength, she was so fragile—feminine and delicate—and in need of his protection. *She was so valuable*, worth his whole kingdom no matter her scarred face or his abject obsession. No Omega anywhere could compare.

"You have my heart, *mon chou*. It might not seem that way when I correct you, or when I make demands, but you own it all the same." Scooping up her limp hand, he pressed it to his bare chest. "Does our bond not tell you so?"

A refusal to answer was answer enough.

"How badly does it hurt?"

Wriggling on her seat, shifting uncomfortably at the

mention of her discomfort, and the why of it, paired with the silent throb on her side of the link.

It had been done. *Necessarily so.* And she had agreed to it—the price she'd named certain to cost him a great deal of conflict with Ancil. Lifting the crystal goblet designed specifically for this vintage of viognier, placing it at the trembling lips of the only thing on the Gods' rotted earth he adored, Jacques urged her to swallow another sip.

She'd been bathed, the water puce and filthy from all he'd been required to wash away. She'd been bandaged. She'd been held close when she sobbed.

She'd been warned.

And though he had spoken his threats with a rational compunction, that didn't change the fact that if the name George crossed her lips again, he'd see the Beta thrown into the most despicable Centrist brothel. To be used until there was nothing left. And Jacques would watch that recording every last hour, over and over, until he was wizened and old.

Against his chest, her finger fluttered, Jacques realizing his thoughts had made him tighten his grip on her bruised wrist. Softening his hand, he nudged her chin. Offering a cajoling, well-meant smile, he pressed a kiss to her scar. "Tell me what will make you smile."

When his mate shrank back from his nearness, sinking inside herself at the brush of his lips, he didn't correct her. Not after what she'd suffered in the bath. "Come now, tell me how to cheer you."

A minute headshake.

She believed there was nothing to remedy her spirit, and that just was not so.

Accept they were at odds and the Omega was unreasonable. He could give her the world. Fine things, the best foods, eternal comfort, endless sexual pleasure.

What she wanted, the only thing her brain focused on, was the very goddamn things he'd forbidden. Which things: Beta rations? Freedom? Ancil's head on a platter? *George*? Further thoughts of the Beta sent his purr to a snarl. Before he could catch himself, he upset his mate all the further.

A mate who was now sobbing into her hands.

Fuck.

When it came to this female, his control had always been less than exemplary. He'd punish himself for that later. *He would do better.*

"Unit 17C, I order you to tell me what you need."

The jolt in her body, he knew to expect. The way eyes, the color of honey in the sun, turned up to meet his eager gaze, Jacques was utterly unprepared for. Steadfast, the fluttering thing in his arms sat taller, grew angry. Drinking him in with the cold eye of a rival, she spoke with harsh tones and great feeling, "I want to hold the baby."

What luck!

Tucking the front panels of her fluffy robe tighter about his mate, Jacques smirked. "Is that all it is?"

Of course! His Omega was upset that she had not fallen pregnant after her first true estrous. How had this not occurred to him? These tears were not due to his attentions during her bath or the deal they'd struck when he bartered his kingdom to wash another male's seed from inside her rectum.

Yes, he'd known she had not understood this request. Yes, he'd manipulated her. And yes, another round of anal penetration had given her pain when there was no estrous to dull it. But his strokes had been cautions, methodical, and slow. And because he loved her more than breath itself, he'd kept his knot outside her sphincter when his excessive ejaculations had rinsed a pathetic rival out of her body.

He'd been exceedingly careful, and she had braced through it like a champion.

Because he'd offered her anything she wanted in exchange. And she had chosen Annette.

And now she wanted to hold the Beta's baby. Jacques pulled her closer and wasn't sure if he could love her more. Precious, brilliant, virginal, and innocent. *His* mate. "Shall I have Annette bring him here now?"

"Now?"

Finally, he's startled her out of her malaise. Watched her tuck the edges of her robe tighter around her bandaged throat and adjust her sore bottom on the soft seat. "Yes, *mon chou*. Now."

Golden eyes darted to the windows, to the night view of his city. They measured, that mind of hers ticking until the feelings that had left her in misery were washed away with logic, with calculations, and with what an Omega should rightfully feel. *Appreciation*.

He thought to please her further. "Upon your next estrous, I'll give you a baby of your own if you want it." He carded his finger through her too short hair. "I suddenly find the idea very appealing."

The idea was ignored, his mate choosing to answer the initial question. Embarrassed as she tried again to use the robe to cover her excessive marks. "Babies sleep at night, do they not? I'd prefer to see him tomorrow."

"First thing. I'll escort you to the nursery."

"Annette will be there?"

"Tending the nursery is her duty. Yes, she will be there."

Like an impenetrable iron wall falling between them, that blossom of hope he'd sensed in his Omega slammed shut. She went utterly cold, eyes fading into unfocused distance. Alpha annoyance reared up to take her enthusiasm's place. "This isn't a fight you want to pick with me, mate. I would have set aside my wife for you in an instant. Don't begrudge any Alpha for loving the other half of his soul."

Irritation. He'd take any emotion over vacancy, and she fed it to him in spades. "You don't have a wife."

"But I do."

Was that jealousy? By the Gods, Jacques latched onto that hint of perfection in his love and held on for dear life as he licked at her ear.

"She's old enough to be my grandmother. We were married when I was fifteen, and the hag never bore children. Bloodlines, and negations, and the prevention of civil war... I wasn't favored heir then, only valuable enough to offer in peace to a rival for my father's power. Once I took that title, she was banished." Sagging breasts and breathy night sighs, Jacques was still repulsed by fair-haired women. "I'll have her removed from the records. You'll be my first wife. Our offspring will rule." Laughing at the inevitability of what would follow, he said, "After they kill one another off for the honor of keeping a hundred-million people alive."

The Omega's face went ashen, her feelings curdling to hear the truth of Bernard Dome's politics. Another thing he'd slowly ease his timid love into.

"It was a joke, *mon chou*." He kissed her nose, pulling her fully into his lap. "I'll make sure the birthing contracts are so solid there can be no usurpers. Our children will know their place and be all the safer for it. Had my father been more cautious, my brother might still be alive."

3

Access to Annette had been bought with an act, unnatural and uncomfortable. Painful.

Estrous had been something unworthy of memory. Something to lock in a box in her mind and never think of, lest she drown in shame.

A bit more pressure in just the right place and she was going to spilt right down the middle.

Yet this male demanded so much. And so soon.

And she was foolish and unprepared for the desires of a Centrist Commodore.

The way Jacques' hand wooed it from her, how he'd murmured and worked to seduce warned her sensibilities to reject such touch. But she could see inside him now in a way that was blinding and overwhelming. And though he asked, cajoled, and purred, no part of him was willing to allow her to deny whatever it was he desired.

On a spiritual level, that's not how he'd been reared.

Unlike her, who'd lived all her years, developed into a perpetual servant of the greater good.

"There are things that can soothe that ache," he'd said. "I don't want his seed inside you. If you let me wash it out, I'll give you anything you want... *within reason.*"

Reason? Logic. Mathematics. Physics. Languages of science constantly blooming in her mind. They had no home in Central or this bond.

Shivering despite the heat of the bath, Brenya latched on to the only thing in this awful place that had ever made her feel good. "I want to visit Annette."

The Alpha's internal debate was loud, though she could make out none of the words. It was loud in his poorly concealed displeasure, in his craving to have his way, in his delusion that all he desired was to please her.

The water surrounding them rippled, the Alpha easing closer. "It's a deal. Now, *mon chou*, brace your hands against the side of the tub and try to relax. Trust me to make it feel good."

This was too easy by half. "I let you touch me and I get to see Annette?"

Reaching for one of the many items ready for his use on the side of the tub, Jacques purred all the louder. "I'm going to do much more than touch you. I'm going to teach you. I'm going to help you know you are mine."

Tiles sweating from so much steam, Brenya put her hands to their slickness and braced.

How mistaken she was.

When his finger prodded the last place she ever wanted to be touched again, it was slimy with something the water did not wash away. Something *soothing, slippery, and chemical.*

Fingers stretched, swished, massaged, and opened her anal opening.

"This was not what I believed you offered."

Soft lips placed a sucking nip on her earlobe, a male chest warming her back. "Is Annette not worth it? I ask so little, you'll see. Relax. I need this. You need this. You just don't understand why."

She didn't need sensitive tissues stretched. She didn't need the reminder that another—a foreign stranger—had been manipulated to penetrate her. All because she was a stupid fool and had not guessed the one called Jules would be sleeping on his ship and not serviced in the palace.

Heart aching for the harm she had caused the Beta, she cried while Jacques cleaned her inside and out. She wept for her mistakes all the while staring at the drips of condensation gathered on the tiles. When his touch retreated and she thought it was over, a sigh left her lips. Only to be chased by a yelp when something thicker, more menacing, and slimed up with that same goo pressed forward. He caught her hips before she might move out of position, and slid his cock through a burning ring despite her squeak of alarm.

"Washed out," he'd said. She should have known better.

Slow, measured thrusts completely opposite of the manic pounding the Beta had given her while her estrous pheromones had drugged him into little more than a rutting animal. Kissed and caressed while Jacques sought his pleasure, he taught her another lesson in what it meant to be Omega.

His pleasure was her pleasure. Her pleasure was easy to cultivate by one as experienced as he.

Climax was unlike the agony of estrous, or the mind-bending false nirvana of vaginal sex. It was something new, incomplete, yet more. Followed by a strong urge to empty out what he flooded her with on a roar.

Alphas came in copious amounts. Jacques seemed to have extra pride in what he could produce.

Orgasm turned to cramping, Brenya's forehead to the sweating tiles as she groaned and felt another belly expanding gush.

So taken was he with what took place between them, when she whined and looked over her shoulder to see how much longer this might last, she found Jacques with his eyes squeezed shut, his head thrown back, and his mouth gaping.

She began to mentally count, watching the play of his complete distraction to her discomfort. Caught up, utterly enraptured with his cock in her ass.

Sliding his hand from her hip, he took his knot and squeezed it with a strength that should have caused him pain, treating this as if it were natural.

And came, and came, and came.

While Brenya counted, felt a pressure too uncomfortable to name.

Fifteen minutes. To the second. That was all she could take before she screamed and struck out.

It wasn't so hard to unseat him, gripping his knot as he

was. Despite the water and the slippery tile, despite what leaked from her open ring right down her leg, she ran to the toilet. Releasing so much more than just his come.

Brenya released real anger at how the world could fill her up—mouth, cunt, anus, heart—perverted by another's charisma.

She released. Warm cream, frothy from the exuberance in which it had both entered and exited her. The scent of semen so strong in the air it almost completely obstructed the scent of blood.

Purging rage, disappointment, frustration, guilt, Brenya did her best to push every last drop of him out of her, knowing exactly what he meant now. His mark had been shot so deep inside it would be leaking out for hours, maybe days considering estrous altered the digestive tract.

This had never been about anal penetration, or sexual gratification. Had it been, Jacques would not have made her endure such copious seed in so unnatural a place.

He was marking what he considered his territory. Marking deep—even though it caused his beloved Omega harm.

And that was telling.

Jacques was threatened by Jules.

An outsider he had tricked into fucking her in the first place.

A foreign dignitary who had a *Rebecca*.

Who must be suffering even more than she at the cruelty of being bound against his will, severed from the female he called out for on the ship, and tied to her.

Tied to Jacques.

Who was a bastard, though he might be beautiful and have all the power in her world.

Epiphanies were not a worthy word for the thoughts that crossed her mind as she sat on that toilet and ignored Jacques refilling the tub. Vendettas did not fit either. Unsure what these feelings were or why they ransacked through her scattering thoughts, she reached out for them. Gathered them close to her heart like a shield.

They were fragments, she considered, of what it must feel like to be a whole person.

The Betas of Bernard Dome had no idea how truly blessed they were.

Unmedicated humanity was hideous. The ways in which she fanaticized about harming a living being brutal.

Burying her head in her hands, another wave of come splattering the basin on a cramp, a final offensive thought broke through all the chaos. One she had to ask before she might throw up. "Are you going to make me have sex with him again?"

That. That one blunt question of her *mate* made him freeze. Every naked muscle flexed as if the creature might burst from his skin, the devil inside seen for what it was.

Alpha anger seasoned ugly air. Yet his back was still to her and his answer had not been given. He asked her a question instead. "Do you wish for the Beta to fuck you?"

Brenya's initial question had in no way signified desire for the Beta, but again, the Alpha who controlled her life spoke with such a snarl it was clear the idea enraged him.

"It would be rape." Of the Beta. But again, Jacques was not understanding the basic level at which she communicated. Brenya wondering again at what she missed here. Unsolved puzzles in a mind like hers would never stop trying to piece together.

Obsessive behavior would follow. It's what had made her an extraordinary grunt.

The toilet began its cleansing function, washing her as it washed itself, the bowl full of filth-spattered come flushing down to the waste process levels to be made into fresh water for drinking, cooking, washing....

"Come to the bath, Brenya. I'll wash it all away."

And so she had, feeling anger, such a raw emotion birthed deep within. And it felt so much better than fear, or helplessness. It got her through that second bath, one where the Alpha wisely kept his cock to himself. It got her through the attention he paid to her every hurt. How after he'd dried her with the softest towels one might imagine, after he set her naked on the bathroom's settee, how he bandaged where two men had bitten her deep enough that the wounds had yet to fully scab.

One bite was clean, one was vicious. The scales between them as if one a scholar and one a madman. One in control and one possessed. Each with their own brand of venom.

Over bruises and sore muscles went silk. White, because Jacques always dressed her in that virginal shade. Hair combed by the deft fingers of a man with longer locks of his own, he spoke to her of mundane things as if they were friends, as if she cared what he might say.

Brenya listened, picking out what might matter—the things between pointless gossip. She listened, because she was enraged, retreating so far inside herself so he could not buoy her up to the calm he preferred… that she found a single quiet corner that even Jacques could not invade.

In that silence, she was not alone.

4

GRETH DOME

"Show me."

Skin instantly pricking to the point it stung, the worst sort of unseen, unheard predator emerged from the shadows. Tired of the constant surprises, Maryanne snarled, "For fuck's sake! Why do you have to sneak up on me like that every goddamn time?"

Isolation had done her few favors. But she breathed, which was more than she could say about the poor saps in Thólos. If they weren't dead now, they would be soon. And those who might still linger? They probably wished they'd died quickly in the siege.

Most of them had been assholes who'd had it coming. She didn't owe them a goddamn thing.

Didn't think about it.

Look forward. Stay alive. Stay in place…

Always in the same three rooms.

This keeping place, *this prison*, the accommodations were larger than her crappy dwelling back in Antarctica. But no windows. Her vitamin D came from specialized lamps and a daily dose of healthy food. She was little more than a tended houseplant.

Unless she suffered punishment, she was ordered to exercise—the regime boring, exhausting, pointless when there was nowhere to go and no city to explore. Not unless she used the faculties left for her amusement.

And by amusement… her only amusement… Shepherd really meant occupation.

Occupation.

On a multitude of levels.

She, an Alpha female of considerable talents, was in prison just as the entire Dome of Greth was unknowingly imprisoned by a tyrant. Yet not once had she tried to escape.

Because she knew exactly what would happen to her. Shepherd had explained it in gory and glorious detail. In a voice so chillingly calm that every hair on Maryanne's body stood on end… and remained so for several days afterward.

And those downy hairs still rose each time the Chancellor of Greth Dome appeared from the shadows like the monster he was.

Prick always liked to sneak up on her. Make his demands. Criticize mistakes. And Gods help her if there was so much as a piece of discarded laundry on the floor.

She couldn't even *live* in her own rooms! What was the point of crisp corners on bedding when it was *her* bedding and she didn't care?

Who scrubbed their bathroom from top to bottom every single day?

No one. No one anywhere did that. And she'd know. She had visual and auditory access to every bathroom in the whole fucking city.

An entire room of her prison was nothing but monitors, feeds, supercomputers, wires, access to anything she might want to look at or hear. But not taste or touch or feel.

Ever.

Lunch had been tomato soup with crackers. Breakfast a bowl of unsweetened oats. Dinner would most likely be some kind of meat, unsalted, unseasoned, unappealing.

While out in the city, there were exotic fruits, local dishes that made her mouth water just to imagine the spices. There was laughter, and drinking, and sex, and fun.

Things meaningless when made to document it all.

Analyze, report. Analyze, report. Analyze, report.

Before she might give the necessary report, a large hand reached forward, the male pointing to one of the many displays of the city. To a market. Adjusting the feed to suit his whim.

Light caught on the gold of his wedding band.

Light dimmed from his eyes.

What he saw in that image. How his expression said nothing. The thoughts that might be going through his head. Maryanne knew better than to guess.

She'd seen that *lack of look* on his face when she'd been imprisoned in the Undercroft. Foreboding, godly, calculating.

And not for her to question.

He had saved her from the worst prison imaginable. She had saved him from Thólos.

And what did she get for it? This perpetual purgatory and fucking tomato soup.

Stuck with an endless surveillance job. Locked away from the sights and smells of an exciting new place.

At least this prison was safe.

No one ever touched her. Not even Shepherd had brushed against her once in all the hours he came and went.

Slave labor, she'd called it, when Jules first dragged her into this... whatever this room was. The bastard Beta had coarsely laughed at her fit, named it salvation.

A sentence with an end date.

Another reason—the reason she pretended to keep her twitching hand off the door—she had not tried to escape.

A girl needed some self-esteem.

Or as Shepherd would preach: a purpose.

To spy.

On every home, every citizen, every transaction, every breath.

Living through the strangers on the screens until many didn't feel like strangers at all. Their names—her favorites at least—she knew. Their preferences in foods, their friends, their favorite sexual position.

Maryanne had access to practically *everything*. Using her tricks to see, to find, to uncover, more and more every day before she went crazy from the solitude. Every last angle of every last room, alley, bedchamber, and communication network. Always watching, now fluent in the local language.

Under grow lamps. Fed bland food. Exercised like a pet. Lonely.

Machines were poor company. Shepherd was worse.

Jules. She hated just enough that verbally sparring with him on the rare occasion he entered her prison gave her something.

Release.

God knew she wasn't having the sexual kind. Unless it was with her hand and maybe acting the voyeur on a particularly interesting liaison.

Yet, being caught masturbating on the job wasn't really the kind of conversation she wanted to have should Shepherd pop out of a dark corner. Which he did if she deviated even slightly from schedule.

So work, work, work.

What the computers missed as they devoured visual and audio data, it was her sole duty to cherry-pick and deliver with a bow and a "sir." To date, Maryanne's reports had resulted in the deaths of four hundred thirty-seven strangers.

Yet Followers didn't just pluck potential insurgents off the street as they would have in Thólos. No bodies were strung from buildings or left to rot in the streets. Here, all was done with finesse. Accidents staged. After all, people slipped off the poorly maintained causeways all the time. Especially before the Queen had returned to save them from themselves.

At Her Royal Majesty Svana's ruling, infrastructure was under repair… but the city was in such poor shape that sometimes buildings collapsed. Maybe while rebel factions happened to be gathered inside. But who cared about settling dust when schools were opened and children were spoiled with knowledge. Hospitals expanded, and the sick recovered. The hydroponic gardens were upgraded, and food became more readily available.

The streets grew safer under the Followers' watchful eyes. After all, criminals knew best how to find their own kind. Squash them like bugs. Take over the necessary rackets. And control everything under the glass.

The economy flourished.

The shy Queen was loved.

The imposing Chancellor Shepherd was adored.

Fact.

Adored, feared. Aggressive and just. A precise blend of politics and power.

All a façade to hide a secret that would bring the city to its knees.

Those under the invader's banner—the Followers dressed in black—had murdered, replaced, discarded, crushed thousands upon thousands of the very people who sang their praises.

And that was fucking terrifying.

As scary as the glint off the gold on his finger and the fact that she was not the only woman locked away in this brightly colored new place. Not once, on any screen, had Maryanne seen Claire.

Report complete, forcing a full breath despite uncanny anxiety, the Alpha female sat a little straighter. "How's Claire?"

Wow, she really was starved for conversation to even dare bring up that name. But the wedding ring… it had been taunting Maryanne for months.

Not just the ring…

The man looming over Maryanne's workstation stank of Claire's slick. Not that Maryanne would dare crack any such joke, or even look at him sideways. Not now. Not ever.

She thought Shepherd had been scary as fuck in the Undercroft. She'd feared him in Thólos. Now, seeing what he'd done in Greth, the man practically made her wet herself.

And here he was, reeking as if he'd come directly from fucking his mate and wanted the world to know it.

"None of your concern."

Death wish. Maryanne had to have had a death wish to ask, "Has she been eating?"

And fuck, she'd caught his full attention. That glacial stare, the weight of so much concentration on a simple living being about to be snapped in half like a twig. Even the way he turned from the dozens of monitors to face her full-on.

Maryanne swallowed.

And Shepherd stared.

Time dragging on like claws on flesh.

A full minute passed. "She's my best friend. Aren't we doing this all for her?"

Cocking a brow, the barest twitch in his cheek, Shepherd verbally struck. "Not once, in all the time she's been safely back in my care, has she so much as breathed your name. Not once, Maryanne."

Chin lifting, Maryanne curled her lip. "Because she thinks I'm dead."

"Does she?" Dismissing her as if she was nothing, gray eyes went back to the monitors. "I think we both know better."

"Why can't you ever be nice to me?" Fire, where it came from, Maryanne didn't know, but it came and burned where she'd been colder than a Thólos corpse. "I follow your orders day in and day out. I obey. I pace, and jump, and wash, and organize. I give you the lives of what might be decent people if they so much as breathe the wrong phrase in passing. What the fuck do you want from me, Shepherd?"

"I want you dead."

Snuffed out, not even a trace of smoke. Frigid, a living corpse. A tired, lonely woman who could really use a drink offered no reply.

Silence was the appropriate response.

With obedience came a sort of mercy. Honesty.

Shepherd, cutting a glance over his shoulder, said, "It frustrates that I can't kill you. Me, because I despise you. You, because you know how close to the grave you will always be. You'll never be a Follower, Maryanne. You're too selfish. Too empty for even me to fill."

"Too useful, you mean."

"You have your uses."

Was that... was that a concession? "I have five more years left in these rooms. I just want to know how Claire is doing."

A flicker of light came to a very dark man. "She is painting today."

Done with her, with her reports, her efforts, her endless toil staring at people free to do as they wished, Shepherd faded back into the shadows. Leaving Maryanne with nothing but her screens.

Dinner arrived. She ate. At the appointed hour, she lay down on her cot, warmed by a colorful blanket in a dreary room.

When the chime woke her so she might slog through another day of endless watching, something new shone like a beacon.

On the wall… a fresh painting of flowers.

For the first time since Thólos fell, Maryanne cried.

And then she threw up.

5

There was dry toast for breakfast.

Maryanne followed protocol: she tidied her sleeping quarters—first cleaning up the drying pool of stale vomit. Afterward, she made the bed with sharp lines. Once bed-making precision had been achieved, she washed her body until her skin stung from the abrasive rag and scentless soap.

Mustering enthusiasm was dreary, her body dragging as she pulled clothing over her limbs.

Entering the arena of her misery—the room of screens—fresh, uninvited tears fell.

Not a single monitor fed her. There was no life to be seen. She had no window…

Maryanne was trapped in a gray prison with nothing but four walls and the lingering stench of barf. There was nothing for her anywhere. An Alpha female who had flouted Shepherd's dominion of Thólos. Who had prepared for a long life of solitude. Who had swept the feet out from under a giant when his mate rebelled. Had nothing.

But dry toast and solitude.

And a painting of flowers she could neither bring herself to look at or avoid.

Lunch was bland tomato soup.

Dinner consisted of... she didn't know. Maryanne had not even looked before she lifted her plate from the slot and sent it crashing against the opposite wall.

"GODS DAMN YOU!"

Two days. No food was sent.

Water, she drank from the tap, its coolness cupped in her palms as she slurped.

On the third day, the darkness lifted. Ten screens came to life.

Only ten.

Each one drab. The display no longer featured the fantastical people of Greth with their bright colors and zest for life. Strange-looking multitudes dressed in gray jumpsuits—characterless, colorless drones going about their day—in a creepy harmony of boring absoluteness.

Two more days, she watched in solitude, forgetting to sleep, to wash, eating her food without tasting as she stared into a mundane, endless caricature of life.

It was sad to see. It was confusing.

The monitors were no longer a game; they were work. There were no trysts or secrets to devour. There was conformity and *peace*.

As if he sensed the moment Maryanne was at her lowest, the darkness parted, and a massive walking nightmare appeared. "Your feed is now keyed to Bernard Dome, located in the former country of France."

France? There had been some information about the place when she'd been the terrible student of her childhood... a history of something? Maryanne could not recall, yet she knew the name and had tuned her ears to the song of a language she did not understand.

Strange as it was, behind the accord and utter boringness of the display, beautiful things made up their architecture and squares. Fountains, cobblestone streets, white, glittering buildings. And she had watched without sleeping. Because the people did not represent the art of the structure. Same haircut, same pasted blandness of expression. Same uniform.

Where were the pickpockets? Where was the lust?

A clock rang, and everyone stood in unison, marched to eat, marched to shit, marched to work, marched to eat.

Did they march to fuck?

Where was that monitor?

A sweet Beta lover she had once been faithful to for over a month had called Maryanne's eyes enigmatic. He had loved her eyes, not just because they were beautiful, but because they were devious. Playful.

Beyond her pouty lips, they were perhaps her best feature.

How long had it been since she'd seen mascara or fluttered her lashes at some potential paramour?

Why did it feel ugly to lift her gaze to acknowledge Shepherd, knowing he found nothing about her appealing? That it didn't matter that her eyes were enigmatic, just as it didn't matter that his whole person was basically disfigured by Da'rin.

Both of them were basically hideous, outward appearances aside.

Acknowledging that for the first time, more than a year into her sentence as Shepherd's indentured prisoner, Maryanne had finally grown a semblance of a spine relating to this man. There was only so much she had left to lose… and it was starting to look more worthless by the minute. "I saved your life in Thólos. I dragged your huge, lumbering body to your men."

As if he might actually be offering comfort, the walking terror put a single hand on her shoulder, reciting a speech as if he had memorized the day they landed on this new ground. "To save yourself and only yourself, Maryanne. Yet I live. Subsequently, Claire lives, so you serve your sentence in luxury. You possess a soft bed outfitted with blankets. From your taps flows clean running water. Unlike your few months in the Undercroft, you have a toilet, a bathing cubical, and a purpose. Daily, you are fed a perfectly balanced diet, delivered to you three times a day, *when you are not unwell*."

If they were going to talk truths, then she had a word or two to add. "I hate it in here."

"Good." Shepherd didn't care, would *never* care about her impulses or her urges. In fact, there was an odd respect for how well they understood one another in that sense. The conqueror, *the king*, held all the power. She held all the resentment. Should she not survive the years of her sentence, Maryanne would die alone, forgotten, with nothing but screens and her hand to see her through.

The idea had flittered through here and there over the ages under Shepherd's thumb. But she had always brushed it off, because there was an end date. There were passions to pursue.

Glorious irresponsibility waited on the other side of that door. She would eat and drink and fuck her way through Greth until the glory of this new place was saturated into her cells.

She would steal things, because she liked to. She would let people down, because it made her remember she was strong.

And some other poor fool locked in a room with screens would watch her every move until an accident cut her down in her prime.

Her useless, pointless, vapid self wiped away as if she had never crossed the ocean on a transport and abandoned her home to desiccate in the arctic snows.

What was she really going to do there? Live in her house while everyone died? Run out of food after a few years of hermit-hood? She was going to wait for a savior to clean up the mess and immerge chubby cheeked and ready to wreak havoc?

She would have died, just like everyone else died. Just a little later.

Completely alone, without so much as a watercolor painting on her wall.

"I won't help you invade another Dome, Shepherd." Wow, had she really just said that?

The weight of his hand still on her shoulder, the man failed to acknowledge her statement. "Impress me, and you will have total control over Bernard Dome surveillance. Fully learn their language. Translation will only be offered by computer for three months. If you fail to attain fluency, these screens shut down forever. You will die in here, well fed, with clean water, withering and pathetic. Exactly how you would have died in Thólos."

Her *host* hit too close to home with that zinger, the first-rate bitch who made her *her* rearing her beautiful head. "My sentence only carries five more years."

She might survive that in solitary confinement. It's not like this Dome was going to be ravaged, cracked, and infested with the virus. She could have made it five years in Thólos too. Though she'd had books and COMscreens. There had been sex toys and distractions.

Shepherd nodded once. "True. Yet, I never claimed that you would leave this room alive. In fact, I have ordered every last Follower to assure that you do not."

Maryanne was not sure when she had looked away from that gray, terrible gaze. Only to look at more gray terrible monotony on the screen. Bernard Dome. "I suppose this is where I mention your mate."

"Maryanne, you are a terrible person. You deserved the Undercroft. Yet I set you free all the same."

She was terrible, through and through. Yet she was also

wise enough to know that somewhere, someone loved her. "Claire would never forgive you."

The magnetism of the man led her to meet his gaze again, right as the scariest Alpha male in creation stated coldly, "Claire would never know."

One Alpha faced off against another, Maryanne rising from her seat to stand tall—her final stand. Words had never worked with this male, the male who had set her free from the Undercroft after unspeakable things had been done to her. Who had set her free to run havoc in Thólos after she begged at his feet for protection. The savior she had abandoned at first opportunity, because he was fucking crazy. The man who had destroyed her enemies and haunted her dreams.

Claire's mate.

The ugliest, most ruthless motherfucker born to a dead world. A beast she had watched murder millions, Maryanne laughing until it wasn't funny anymore.

A male who did not flinch when her forearm swept her workstation, sending instruments flying before she might button down real rage. "What more do you want from me, Shepherd?"

Never one for subtlety, a massive hand fit over the top of Maryanne's skull—turning her gaze to a new illumined screen.

The new world of… nothing that already led her eyes to unfocus.

Because demeaning her seemed to be one of his greatest sports, Shepherd spoke to her in a tone that let her know precisely how much of a simpleton she was. "You are worthless as you are. So grasp this. *Jules* requested that I spare your life. Therefore, I keep you."

Well, leave it to the ol' creepy blue-eyed Beta. "Jules, huh?"

"Any allegiance you might have in those hollow bones belongs to him." Shepherd flipped on another monitor, in such a way that it was utterly embarrassing to realize she could have turned them on herself at any time. "So I suggest that you pay attention to these screens and see what you have failed to notice in the last two days."

No way! No way was Jules in a cell in some eerie foreign Dome!

There was something, something almost human in Shepherd's statement. "Should he die, Maryanne, so shall you."

Jules, the cryptic, nasty piece of shit that he was sat unmoving on the newly illuminated eleventh screen. Solitary in a cell that lacked even a toilet. A cell nowhere near as nice as hers.

Her Jules, her only tie to civilization.

"I don't... I don't understand." Why in the heck was he even on foreign soil?

"You will report on the hour, every hour."

"What about sleep?"

"Every hour until you can give me something worth keeping you alive. Apply your talents—"

"My Gods! Is that porn projected on his cell wall? What the...? Why are they showing him...? Wow... that Alpha could use some pointers. Did you see how—"

"It is a live feed, which you will find on screen seventy-two. Meet Jacques Bernard, the regent of Bernard Dome and his Omega, Brenya Perin. I would like to know why Jules' tenure in their prison involves watching the Omega suffer."

"Gross. Look at her face, she's mangled." Maryanne was already totally sucked in, speaking to herself when she muttered, "Someone get that girl a sandwich. Oh, and some backbone. Did you see that? She's not even fighting anymore. Who treats their mate that way?"

"Yes, I see it."

"It's just wrong… she's crying."

"Every hour, Maryanne. On the hour. Or all the screens go dark, your food dries up, and all you will have left as you starve is the painting to remind you of how horrible you truly are." And like that, he was gone.

Every hour, on the hour, she sent a report, unsure what Shepherd was looking for, but scandalized by what she found as she switched on more screens.

Bernard Dome was more fucked up than she was.

And that was saying a lot.

6
BERNARD DOME

Two china teacups, their golden rims catching afternoon sunlight, sat on saucers so intricately detailed that Brenya stole a longing glance in their direction. There wasn't much time, which left her with no opportunity to admire the mathematical precision of hand-painted patterns. Right there on a silver tray sat true engineering, crafted many centuries before the Red Consumption ravaged the world. Art sculpted, painted, and lacquered by persons—not a fabrication machine. A simple brush held by a master. A precious treasure.

Right there.

So fragile it was uncanny.

Yet, more fragile was the woman rising to greet her.

High ceilings, frescos of playful cherubs painted onto the opposite wall. Gold finishings, damask curtains, polished wood, the scent of fresh flowers. It seemed the perfect place, positioned, adorned, *landscaped*—if you will—to showcase the slumbering baby in an elegantly carved cradle just so.

The entirety of the room had been fashioned to draw the eye to chubby cheeks and long eyelashes. To the gentle snores of a tiny human.

As if Brenya might not notice the two Beta attendants who tried and failed to become part of the architecture.

She stared at them more than she stared at the child, pausing in her rush forward to drink down every detail concerning the uninvited pair.

Just as the room was beautiful, just as the waiting table was beautiful, the servants—both female—were beautiful. Each with their matching, crisp white aprons and dedicated expressions of disinterest.

This was not what Brenya had paid dearly for. Another reminder that Jacques twisted his promises and took as he pleased.

Those two had no place in this moment.

They didn't belong in the room of a mother and her child. Sentinels… spies.

Touching the uncomfortable lace at her throat, Brenya gave the constrictive garment a tug. Wincing when fabric cut into the concealed bite made by a rabid dog.

So much artifice.

What did it matter if the lace and silk of Brenya's dress was soft? The fabric covering bruises and aching bite marks in pure white lied. It confined, rubbed where she ached—a constant reminder that she had been claimed roughly, used horribly.

Nervous fingers went from tugging at her too tight collar to smoothing back fallen strands of hair. She had rushed, and the bound-up mass held with a comb of glittering stones had slipped. Surprise, the most idiotic way to confine hair imaginable failed should she move at anything but a glacial pace.

Jacques had dressed her to his tastes. Meticulous, his fingers had been careful with each button down her spine. He'd drawn a brush through her hair as if the lightest tangle might leave her in tears.

Yet he had confined her in misery and inconvenience.

And then he had deemed it was time jewelry should be considered. Would Brenya be willing to pierce her ears? "Just a quick prick," he'd said, fleeting pain that could be soothed as quickly as it came.

Her resounding "no" inspired the Alpha to cock a brow.

Which meant she had already lost.

The Commodore's promises, interpretations, and manipulations—his way of *asking by taking*.

He may have been wallowing in his conquest, their pair-bond, and the joy it brought to his being, his feelings may have overshadowed all she was, but for a moment, her distrust and resentment were greater. She hated when he asked her opinion as if it might matter or alter his course.

She hated it.

Sour feeling poured right out of her into him, a choking miasma of uncontrolled anger. The homunculus of her rage grew as if a physical thing. Rising to stand over her, the look of shock upon his face had been followed by a sneer..

He reached out as if he was going to touch her... again...

and Brenya fell into full retreat.

Eyes narrowing, the Alpha's purr ceased—a vulnerable moment between surprise and defensiveness, which gave him away. Jacques Bernard, Commodore of Bernard Dome, would ultimately destroy her.

All the sooner if she could not rein in her disgust.

She took a deep breath, composed herself, and relaxed her jaw. As did the monster facing her.

"I'll ask again, Brenya. May I pierce your ears?" He touched her immediately, as if nothing untoward had passed between them. Gently stroking her hair, Jacques offered what some might consider a timid flirtation. "I have jewels more ancient than old Paris rotting to the north. They would shine like your eyes."

Much calmer, Brenya repeated her refusal. "No."

Male fingers toyed with her earlobe, massaging the flesh as the Alpha considered. "Queens wear their king's jewels, *mon chou*."

"You are not a king. You are a Commodore." And a male whose eyes she could no longer bear to meet.

"Why, today, must everything be negotiated or bought?" The forceful wave of Jacques' frustration battered against the fragile wall between his presence and where she tried to find a place of her own. "I am your Alpha, you are my Omega. Trust in your design to follow where I lead. Your ears should be pierced so I can give you gifts."

She had let him dress her, tend her wounds, press his kisses to her skin, paint her face, style her hair. She'd eaten from his hand, submitted to his perversions. She had followed, because she was utterly trapped in the prison of him. But this, this hill she was willing to die on.

They were *her* ears, and he'd already put enough things in her. "No, thank you."

"Brenya, I swear to you that loving me will come easily and naturally if only you would surrender." Fingers trailed down her arms until Jacques swept her hand into his. Holding them to his heart, he smiled beautifully. An inner radiance burned where the link forcefully pulled between them, searing through her dark disinterest.

As if set aflame, her sad barricade burned to ash under his influence. Expression crumpling into anguish, she shook under his touch and fell open to him in the most intimate of ways.

"There you are, *mon chou*." Kissing her fingertips, Jacques smiled. "Like a frightened bird in my hand, wings fluttering as it learns to be tame and trust."

He wasn't wrong. Whatever part of her he touched through the link was flailing, grasping desperately for peace or apathy that was slipping out of reach. It was as if there were two of her. Or perhaps, just one of her that was being ripped right down the middle. It was either concede or lose herself totally.

So that comforting darkness was stolen away when self-preservation trumped desire. Her splitting, battered psyche gave up its sad, clawing attempts at succor before it was broken completely like an over-loved toy.

Better the body than the mind.

And this Alpha had done ghastly things to her body. He

would do them again. His arms had already swept her into an embrace. He purred with renewed vigor—a loud rattle that shook off the greater part of her desperation.

And all she could offer to combat the utter enormity of what made up Jacques Bernard was a mournful, pathetic croon. "Leave one part of me the way I was before."

The weight of his long sigh was nothing to the weight of his internal annoyance. "We will discuss the topic at another time. More importantly, dear mate, perhaps this isn't a good day for you to meet with Annette."

"You promised."

"Brenya...."

Her façade cracked, the desperate *bird* he described fluttering against its cage as she hid her face in his shirt. "I let you do what you did, because you promised I could see Annette. What worth is your word?"

How strange it was. Insulting him verbally, he ignored. The Alpha was only focused on the incongruous link. Going so far as to wave off her statement, he went back to tucking her hair into the combs. "She won't be the Annette you remember. I have caught up on every report. The Beta rations have been extremely effective. Let me find you a new companion."

The wave crashed—the rage. It broke, it led to a curled lip and a deeply satisfying snarl. "You *lied* to me."

Pure male, the Alpha narrowed his gaze. "A short visit then. Tea. One hour as our room is cleaned." Conceding, Jacques pulled away, kneeling so he might place shoes on her feet. "And while you are there, I shall devise other entertainments for you. Lady Annette is not a suitable companion now—"

"—now that you are poisoning your childhood friend with Beta rations?"

An impatient flutter of Jacques' fingers, a jump of muscle in his cheek. "You must spend time with the other mated Omegas. That includes Ancil's pregnant mate, Lucia. As complications have arisen since her arrival, she lacks your freedoms and is lonely for company. I understand the circumstances of her appearance upset you, but you are a compassionate woman. It is not her fault Ancil recognized his mate. Nor is it her fault that she enthusiastically embraced him. Just as it's not Annette's fault that she made the mistake of loving her husband. The contract they signed was exceedingly clear."

Centrist society made no sense. It served no purpose Brenya might grasp. "Was it her fault for loving you as her friend?"

"My sweet Omega, you are as vulnerable and as new as a fresh born calf. Wide eyed, on shaky legs, easy for any predator to devour were it not for the herd. I can assure you that after a year of experience as my mate, you will feel far differently than you do today."

What a horrible thought. "If that should be the outcome, then I would deserve you."

A passionate yet soft kiss fell on her lips. He breathed in her scent as he agreed, "Yes, dear Brenya."

Glittering shoes, the heel low, encased feet hidden by a long skirt. Aching all over, yet every mark hidden, Brenya took a step back, wiping her skirt as if there was beloved engine grease on her hands, as she said, "May I go to Annette now?"

"You've underestimated me, Brenya. So many times. I am Commodore, *King*, because I took power from the brother I murdered. I fed an Omega to Ancil when he looked at you too long. I faced down a true despot and now hold his envoy in prison. Yet you think I cannot see your every transparent scheme. *Your mind is brilliant.* You were born with a genius I admire beyond words, yet you have been overcome time and again by the Alpha you belong to. So, hear me, my darling mate, when I say to you that I am not blind to your intentions."

The sorriest part of it all… Brenya had none. Her every response since she'd been rescued had been unthinking and erratic. She was chafe in the wind. Utterly lost yet blown around.

Employing that same gentle tone, that overwhelming purr, Jacques took her chin between his forefinger and thumb. "Annette does not belong to you. You can't keep her."

She thought of George and how horribly he had been ripped away.

And it was as if Jacques could read her very thoughts. "If you speak his name, you know what I will do to him."

Brenya would never speak the name of her friend and savior again. Nor would she underestimate the intelligence of the slavering Alpha who had countered her every move. "Please, I just want to see Annette."

The sound of grinding teeth was short-lived. "There is no

need to look at me that way."

But that look, whatever it may have been, drew the terrible Alpha to escort her down glittering halls to a door guarded by no less than five Alpha soldiers. The portal parted, which led to a room boasting nothing more than sunlight and a circular table holding a large vase filled with blooms.

At Brenya's back, the doors closed. She was alone in a scented, pretty passage, the door waiting ahead painted the appealing green of moss.

Though he was no longer standing over her, Jacques' irritation pounded at her breast. Brenya ignored it, opened that door... to find a room the gentle color of sunlight through a soft cloud. Ivory warmth. Brightly colored, beautiful things.

The intricate rug under her feet had been woven in shades of green that lent the room a sense of life. Of the forests outside the Dome, of the wild things that grew in abandon.

Two Beta observers and an Annette whose smell left Brenya salivating for Beta rations.

Standing from her chair, Annette offered a cloth napkin. "You're bleeding through your lace."

Her neck, yes. Brenya could feel the ragged bite mark there oozing. And it was liberating to know she ruined the dress Jacques had spent so long trapping her in.

But there were teacups to consider. Intruding Betas to analyze. There was a sense of unbelievable longing and extravagant relief at seeing Annette unharmed.

And there was the true, hideous honesty of the situation.

So Brenya rushed forward to and embraced the Beta.

7

Annette returned the affection with restrained dignity.

The Beta did not complain at the crushing hold of a desperate Omega, at the comfort Brenya sought and —unpracticed in the sport—tried to return.

She didn't complain or coo; she didn't pet or push away. Annette allowed unladylike clinging, gently patting a very troubled young woman's back as Brenya struggled to find words.

Annette even spoke first. "It's so good to see you, Brenya."

Unsure, Brenya puzzled out if that might be true. How could this feeling be good? Was that what good was supposed to be in Central? Was it a frantic mishmash of bangs and pings colliding within the cage of her ribs? Was it the awkward inability to steady her breath as she clung to someone who had been horribly mistreated?

Was good that small spark of relief despite all the wrong?

Was it that little flicker that began to burn brighter despite the ugliness of her day?

Seeing Annette felt… maybe like hope.

A lot like despair, because she might never get to see her again. Because Alpha arms could reach in at any moment and tear them apart.

As if she knew just what to do, the Beta rocked her gently—like the wind that had blown Brenya's body back and forth against the Dome after she had fallen. Tangled in those ropes, no matter the pain or the hopelessness of that situation, there had been white flowers and fresh air, and that gentle sway in the breeze.

All of it had smelled sweet.

Annette smelled sweet, and it wasn't just the poison of Beta pharmaceuticals.

A few more seconds in her arms and Brenya had her answer. "Yes, Annette. It is *good* to see you."

At that, the Beta began to gently pull away, setting her attention to the little marks of blood blooming on the lace circling Brenya's neck. "Estrous went well?"

"No." It could not have gone more wrong or felt more degrading. No part of Brenya was capable of comprehending how anyone would desire such a thing. "It was awful. Jacques did things. I'm… ashamed."

With a gentle squeeze of Brenya's hand, Annette said, "You tried to escape, and you were punished. It was the

Commodore's duty to correct you. The Beta women of Central know it is best to accept Alpha authority. I have told you this, Brenya. We all must work within the confines of our station and situation. Running will never solve any problem, it only creates more. Promise me you won't do it again."

"There is nowhere to go, Annette. I know that now."

How horrible it was to admit that certainty aloud. Even if Ambassador Havel had lied about the state of Thólos, to leave would start a war that Jacques had stated he could not win. An Alpha, an arrogant, haughty, egotistical Alpha with all the power, had admitted to her that he would lose and her people would suffer. Feeling his consciousness intermeshed with hers, she knew the male had not lied.

"Not every situation will be easy to swallow. The role of wife is the most unrewarding and perilous assignment under the Dome. We must find our joy in motherhood."

"Swallow?" A particularly odd choice of words, considering.

Annette had swallowed Beta rations without question. She had been cast aside and reduced to a simple cot tucked mostly out of sight in her child's light-drenched nursery. The Beta's sleeping place pointedly unadorned, with nothing but a thin blanket, a small pillow—half hidden behind a screen. A sad corner that paled in comparison to the grandeur of the glittering nursery with its cheerful ivory walls and clean, perfect furnishings.

Yet, which of them was more miserable?

Not the drugged Beta who had accepted the poison and

even told Brenya not to interfere when she'd spoken up before the Alphas in power.

Brenya was hanging on by a thread, and Annette was… surviving.

In the confines of her station and new situation.

"You're at a disadvantage, Brenya. I had an entire lifetime of training to assume the role of wife." The Beta untangled herself from Brenya's arms, gesturing for her guest to take a seat at the table. "And while the training was rigorous, I had a loving mother to guide me. *You* were farmed and indoctrinated to work without question. Your duty was folded into you in an environment designed and administered almost without flaw. I doubt you even realize you are now the most powerful female in Bernard Dome."

Brenya moved toward the chair Annette had prepared for her. Wincing at the soft pillow when there would be no comfortable position, considering the part of her body Jacques had just invaded, she fought her skirts so her legs were not strangled.

"Don't let them see that you are in pain. Everyone will take note." With perfectly manicured nails on soft hands that had never seen hard labor, Annette lifted a silver teapot. Steaming mahogany-colored liquid filled each cup, the movement of the hostess practiced, effortless, and… lacking her stolen luster. "Have your tailors slit your skirts until you learn how to properly arrange them. And smile. You don't have to mean it."

Stiff, Brenya offered Annette the very smile the sweet

Beta had taught Brenya only weeks before. It faded as quickly as it came, an unsustainable lie.

Their eyes met as Annette passed her the saucer and cup, their gazes held. On a blink, Annette spilled a single tear. One she ignored as if it had never happened. And then she smiled, her dazzling, practiced smile... and it almost felt real.

"Your tea will get cold, Brenya."

So the Omega sipped, finding the hot beverage overly sweet.

"You taste honey." Annette took a delicate draw from her cup. "An extra spoonful should always be added for when the Alphas are rough."

Rough was not near enough to describe what Centrist Alphas were.

Brenya took another, deeper swallow.

"This blend was specially prepared to soothe your aches and lighten your spirits. Rosehip, turmeric, ginger... my mother's recipe. She made it for me the morning after my wedding night."

"What is a wedding night?"

"It's when the transfer of your ownership moves from your parents to your husband. It's the moment past the contracts and negotiations and physical pleasure, where you bear the true weight of an Alpha for the first time. Tradition demands that the following morning, there is a breakfast only married women might attend. Usually, it's a pleasant affair of comfort, congratulations, advice, and sweet stories."

"And when it's unusual?"

Another practiced smile, this time accompanied by a

small plate of square foodstuffs. "When it's unusual, extra honey is added to the tea. Occasionally, a ranking male relative might petition parliament for marital negotiations on behalf of their kin. This is a miniscule proceeding, filed once, and usually forgotten. In Central, it is bad manners to formally interfere with another's wife so long as the marriage contracts are upheld."

Brenya had been taught her whole life that Bernard Dome was a society of equality and freedom, where all who lived under the glass worked in harmony for the greater good. Tens of millions of citizens believed that lie, they even enjoyed their ignorance. It seemed, despite their current circumstances, Annette's life had been far uglier… and would get uglier still.

Her friend felt almost nothing. Brenya felt entirely too much.

And there was nothing to be done for it but sip tea and drink in the moment before it was gone forever. "I don't know what it means to be the most powerful woman in Bernard Dome."

Because surely she was powerless.

Annette set down her empty cup. "It means, sweet Brenya, that you can have as much honey as you want."

"Annette… I'm sorry."

Blue eyes as pretty as the sky outside the Dome did not glitter with amusement, playfulness, or energy for life. They did not glitter at all. "I understand now why you begged for Beta rations. Honey only goes so far."

Throat bobbing from a nervous swallow, Brenya set down

her too sweet tea, silently agreeing that the honey would never be enough. "Annette, everything you're saying to me, he will hear. I'm sure he's even watching."

"The Commodore? Of course he is watching. He sent the honey."

It was hard to even speak his name. "Ancil, Annette. Your husband."

"No." She shook her head. "Ancil is not watching. There is nothing in this room of worth to him." A feminine wave gestured toward the two silent Beta attendants, in their matching dresses and pinafores. "Not that they won't report to him later. But if he has any questions, they will center on your behavior today, not mine."

Failing to glance at the attendants, Brenya drank in the blue eyes of her friend. Eyes that seemed much wiser than she had ever shown herself to be. "And what will they say?"

"That, though you acknowledged estrous, you have failed to mention your new pair-bond. That you appeared emotionally unstable. That you ate and drank all that you were given. That you squirmed in your seat and picked at your cuticles. This will please him. He will not want you to outshine his new Omega. Lucia's performance in a social situation would have been flawless."

It wasn't flippant. It wasn't rude. It wasn't bitter. Annette was simply matter of fact.

Brenya had missed the honesty of Beta conversation, so much so that the soft smile on her mouth was genuine. "Then they can tell him that I didn't mention the pair-bond, because

I didn't come here to talk about Jacques. Jacques talks about himself enough."

Reaching for the teapot to refill their cups, Annette offered a simple "I know why the Commodore fell in love with you."

"I don't understand what 'in love' is supposed to mean, but whatever it is you felt for Ancil, that is not what the Commodore feels for me." Eyes going out of focus, Brenya stared into the middle distance, poorly trying to explain the horror in her chest, the gnawing, unwelcome savagery, the endless intrusion. "It's a hunger that will never be satisfied. And it will keep eating me until I am dead. It has no consideration for my life. I don't really exist to it. I'm just the trough where it feeds. And it hurts, Annette, far more than falling from the Dome did."

"And to think, I desired to be an Omega more than anything else in the world." There it was, another brief flash of grief that no amount of Beta rations would ever fully quell. "Maybe Ancil would have loved me back if I was."

"I'll love you instead." Just as she loved the Dome and the good people laboring within it. "I'll love you, even if he never lets me see you again."

"The Commodore won't." There was no emotion in Annette as she confirmed what Brenya felt echo as true through the pair-bond. "You made a grave mistake when you walked through the door. You forgot that you were here to hold my baby."

A wash of cold dread chilled Brenya to the bone. She stumbled for an explanation, because *he was watching*, and he was calculating, and she had poorly tried to manipulate and failed. She made herself look at the child in the cradle. One conveniently positioned right beside her. Rosy, chubby cheeks, the tiny nose, and puckered lips. "Your son... is asleep."

"Yes, sedated so he wouldn't cry in your arms." Looking down at her child, Annette reached out a hand to gently rock his cradle. "The tiny thing cries constantly, since he's been denied my breast. I can't risk it, you see."

Because of the Beta rations.

Staring down at her son, Annette smiled. "I told you, wives find our purpose in our children. I have never seen anything more perfect than my son."

Brenya couldn't follow where this conversation had gone. "Jacques told me that your parents held important positions and—"

Still rocking the cradle, Annette confirmed what Jacques had said. "They have *very* important positions, positions that could petition parliament and be heard. Which is precisely why I have forbidden them from entering this room. Neither my mother nor father may touch my son. Because I know what they will say." The cradle continued to sway, Annette's focus completely on her sleeping child.

Something was very wrong here, Brenya wishing she understood the nuisance of conversation. "What will they say, Annette?"

"To forget. To allow my son to slip away. They would make promises that my marriage contract might be dissolved and a new husband provided. Yet Ancil would never bear an *unwanted complication* to restrict his Omega's offspring's legacy. If I leave this room, my son will die."

This is what Annette had been trying to convey from the beginning, but Brenya was too stunted to understand. And now that she'd had to say it straight, there would be so many consequences for everyone who had sipped honey-laced tea. "So you are working within the confines of our station and situation, which is why you ate the Beta rations and told me not to interfere."

"His name is Matthieu, and I refuse to forget him."

8

GRETH DOME

There was nothing that had ever existed or that might ever exist like the feel of his Omega's cunt choking his cock for seed. Vocal—because it was safe to fully let go in this home he had prepared for them—Shepherd let out guttural groan, praising her, in harmony with her cries of pleasure.

Like the sucking kiss of the best-trained whore. The rippling grip of soft hands squeezing the life from the neck of their prey. A slick-drenched sleeve that had been shaped to accept a cock he knew was intimidating in size. The woman who possessed such powers drained his tightly drawn balls until there was not a drop left to wring out.

While she screamed his name. While she bit, scratched, undulated, and prayed.

Her body stripped him bare, forced his climax, drank his seed. Her body craved.

At long last, his little one *craved*.

The way they fucked in the mornings now, it wasn't perfunctory, it wasn't out of a sense of her fear or his duty to remind her of who she was. It wasn't because he pressured her to enjoy sex. It was because his little one woke *hungry*. And Shepherd had the bite marks to prove it.

His mate was starved.

For him, for his company, for his affection, as if the cloud was finally lifting. She could see him, he could embrace her. They even… played.

He had never played before.

Men like him had not been designed for such things, yet he gave that experience to her, no matter how foreign or unlikely it might be. After all, he had not destroyed Thólos and conquered Greth—he had not carved out a new world—intending to sit on the side and watch others experience freedom while he did not.

Shepherd was going to take this life by the throat and know its pleasures, train himself to understand them. With the help of a rambunctious Omega. A healing female who had defeated her addiction to the flood of narcotics she had been given in Thólos—powerful drugs he had seen strong men fall to. And she had done it unaware of what she swallowed or why.

She wanted to feel normal, she had told him, so that she could feel his love. It was worth more to her than a perpetual high or the false safety of chemically induced apathy.

Claire O'Donnell, who fought daily to face her demons and gain ground against them.

Who was finding joy... with *him*.

Knowing that the Gods truly favored him—that beyond all likelihood, his Omega had been delivered to his lap on the brink of estrous. Never would Shepherd regret a single moment of forcing their bond, of taking what the world owed him.

He possessed the perfect woman because when the opportunity presented itself, he acted.

And stole her from the world.

Once he had her, he learned as all mated Alphas must, that he knew nothing of what a pair-bond truly signified.

No wonder Alphas sold their souls to possess such a thing. No wonder they stole. No wonder they rose up from the Undercroft foaming at the mouth in their craving to gather their mates.

Claire might always resent how it was done, that the females matched to his Followers had no choice in the matter.

Such things were kept from her eyes now. And the violence of Thólos had evolved into the cunning of Greth. Here, Omegas were plentiful. They registered proudly and were flagrant with their freedoms. Chosen by unbonded Followers as simply as browsing a catalogue.

Rarely were they taken by force, not when they could be wooed openly and competed for. There had been four registered fights to the death between his men. The victor claimed the Omega—who was blissfully unaware of the goings on between the males.

One of those situations had gone wrong. The Omega

preferred the dead rival and found herself unexpectedly bonded. Mistakes had been made with the Follower's keeping of her, which required diligence and effort to correct.

Shepherd understood, perhaps better than any other, and offered counsel that—had Claire heard it—would have left her weeping in rage.

Ultimately, Shepherd was correct, and the Omega was learning there was more to a match than the beauty of her partner.

A thriving pair-bond required an Alpha willing to invest the effort. To affect diligence in cultivating their mate. They required an Alpha willing to both adapt from mistakes and compel resistant Omegas.

Fuck her until she couldn't remember her name. Watch her mannerisms and learn who secretly lived behind the façade. Feed her well. Dedicate time to the attention she may not want but her dynamic craved. At the slightest hint of progress, double down. Overwhelm her.

Claire was thriving under such ministrations. She bloomed when Shepherd obliterated her boundaries.

As her therapy progressed, the more he unleashed—teasing out her primal possessiveness, using her body, her chemistry, her pheromones against her until she was forced to meet a side of herself that she tried to forget.

The warrior who had dared defy him in Thólos.

The girl who had shared images of her naked body with her people in an attempt to incite insurrection.

The indomitable, determined adversary that she conveniently tried to tuck away now that the world had made her wiser.

Claire's self-enforced seclusion was unnatural to her healing spirit.

Just as dancing with her to the music of his new kingdom was unnatural to Shepherd's entire life experience. Yet he did it, pulling her to him. Drawing out her giggles as they stumbled through steps, bodies touching in a way if she ever touched another male, that male would be a very dead man.

He told her so. She was only permitted to dance with *him*. And that had made her laugh all the harder.

It had made her run her hands down the sides of her body, turn, and flash him a coquettish smirk. He could not be held responsible for the rug burn on her knees. Or the ruins of her clothes.

His little one knew she was toying with fire.

She was testing herself too.

Yes, there had been a great deal of fear in the air when he took her down and stole her wind. Feral, he had ripped apart her clothes, roaring until he uncovered a nipple and fell upon it.

She had told him to stop, and he had fucked her twice as hard to drive home a monumental point.

If she tempted, he would devour.

There would be no more cautious couplings. Not when he knew what she could take.

And she could take it all.

Down her throat, stuffed in her cunt, the most obscene things he might imagine. He'd danced with her, then indulged the wanton Omega slut Claire pretended didn't live behind fluttering lashes and soft conversation.

The nest was no longer just her place to hide. It was his place to defile. She wanted it tidy, he purposefully disrupted her design as he threw her body about and rutted until her outrage at his rudeness had been fucked right out of her.

Claire had thought to argue with him about it over breakfast.

Shepherd responded by hiking her up under his arm in the exact manner he had done the first time they had met in the Citadel, dragging his spitting mate back to her freshly made nest, and destroyed it over a series of hours while he fucked her until her pupils were so blown she could do nothing but gush slick. A mighty knot had sent her into a tailspin of excitement, irritation, desire, pleasure, anger, and while he had her pinned where there was no escape, he lifted the nearest pillow and ripped it right down the middle until a shower of feathers had left the room coated in downy white.

It was her only warning. It was his victory. And it was a sign it was time to overwhelm her. "We do not politely couple in bed, little one. We make love, and our love is not soft, or gentle, or sweet. It is vicious, eternal. It has teeth and claws. When I fuck you, at no time will my attention be on the placement of your pillows—unless I put that pillow under your hips so I can fuck you even deeper. You want a pretty nest like you see on COMscreen articles? Build it, knowing that I will leave it in ruins as I do things to you in it that will leave you screaming my name."

The flush in her cheeks after his statement, the tightness

of her nipples... she hated that his vulgarity excited her. Because it wasn't done out of cruelty or disregard. It was done because to him, nothing mattered more than her ultimate pleasure. If she was distracted by silk and satin, then she was wasting thought that should be on them.

Her *only* focus when she dared tease him with a wicked lick of her lips should be taking the pleasure her beast would give her.

A little line grew between her brows. An expression Shepherd could read like a book. Just as he knew she was about to look to the side and sigh before she spoke.

"Sometimes, I want you to be soft."

Rolling to his back, despite the feathers, he laid her on his chest in the position she loved best. And Shepherd gave her soft in the way she really desired it. With gentle touches and luxurious purrs. He soothed all her aches. When the knot diminished, he pulled her body so she might straddle his face, and contentedly lapped between her legs—a shiver going down his spine to feel her little hands burrow into his hair as she took her pleasure.

A shiver. A sensation he had never felt before Claire. Before Greth.

That shiver... he would go to any length to know that shiver under her touch.

She came with his tongue strumming her clit, his fingers buried deep and rubbing the nerves that sought a knot. Eyes glowing, jaw loose, and breath shallow, Claire let go.

And he considered the lesson complete.

The sleepy sex-drugged smile that followed left the link singing in the perfect pitch of Omega joy.

And it lasted a few seconds longer each day.

"I love you."

Tucking herself against his side as if she might tempt him to laze about with her all day, she offered a contented murmur. "I know you do, Shepherd."

Carding his fingers through silken black hair, he purred. "And you love me."

It was not a question, nor did it require an answer. It was fact.

Snickering, she put a hand to her cheek and closed her eyes.

There was little he loved more than her natural laugh. "What is funny?"

Still snickering, she said, "This morning, I added a banana to your green sludge and some local spice I can't pronounce. According to my COMscreen, beyond its excellent flavor, it is favored by wives to calm their overly sexual men."

Cocking a dangerous brow, he took her chin and met wickedly dancing green eyes. "You want me to be less sexual?"

She bit her lip, playful, before she teased, "I wanted you to stop destroying my nests. I suppose next time I should double the dose."

Such cheek earned her a light swat on her ass, which only turned her giggles into outright laughter.

"The room will be cleaned and fresh bedding provided.

Fluff your pillows to your heart's content after your language lesson."

"I build the nests for you." Letting her fingers trace the definition of his abs, she hummed, content in his arms. "I can tell that you've been tense lately, and I've made an extra effort to create somewhere comfortable for you to relax. Which makes me wonder... why don't I plan a fun distraction since my nest genius hasn't hit the mark? There's this film..."

The predatory kind of stillness came over the Alpha. "I'm listening."

"Beyond my love of nest design"—she gave him a little poke—"and, yes, I know you have been spying on my COMscreen history, *creep*. I have been watching local films to work on my language skills... which I know you also know, as every one of my instructors tells you everything I do."

There was no point in denying it. "They do."

"Very cute, Shepherd. Now, hear me out. From my lessons on the culture here, I learned that it's considered a pleasure to watch the films outside, projected on a wall. Fresh air, cocktails... a common community event.

His hands stopped petting her back, Shepherd's focus exact. "You wish to be outside, in a crowd, at night?"

She leaned up to meet his gaze, black hair spilling over his broad chest. "I was thinking something more intimate. There is a wall in our garden. That nook in the corner where I like to read. I can make us a nice dinner and set up a place for us to relax and try this Greth experience."

"No, little one."

She gave up with no bluster, a blend of disappointment and relief on her face. "You're right. It was a silly idea. It's not safe to be outside when it's dark."

"Your film will need to be displayed at another location."

Her eyes widened. "Wait. What?"

Cupping her cheek, he purred and stroked... made a show of deliberation. Yet there was no deliberation, this move on the board had been orchestrated over weeks. Every last article or fragment of information allowed on her COMscreen hand-selected by him for a series of potential outcomes. Bait to draw her out of their home. "There are others who might enjoy this film and festivity. You are correct. We should embrace the Greth custom."

Lips lightly pursed, shallow breaths a clear sign of anxiety, Claire stammered, "That... no. That is not—"

Untangling their limbs, he began to stand up and make ready for the day. "What film is it that you wish to see, little one?"

It was clear she didn't fully grasp how greatly she had been outplayed. "It's about a baker. I can't remember what it's called."

The very film he had chosen for her and assured popped up in "advertisements" as she scrolled through her articles on local nesting styles.

Pleased with himself, yet above gloating, Shepherd declared, "I will ask my men if they have heard of a popular film about a baker. And I will also have subtitles prepared. You are not the only one still learning the language."

Slipping from the bed as if to chase him down through all the feathers before he might escape, she said, "That sounds like an awful lot of work. It was a silly idea. I know you are busy. We should stay here where it's quiet."

It was time to make his intentions clear. "I want to see this film about a baker and try this Greth custom. I want to do this with you."

"In front of other people?" Pinging suspicion knocked from her side of the link, Claire trying to intimidate him with the idea of normalcy in an effort to escape it herself. "You would dance with me and laugh and *relax* in front of your men?"

Towering over her as he pulled on his shirt, Shepherd shot her a smirk. "I came here to have a life, Claire. Many would relish an opportunity for some simple entertainment with their partners."

And now his perfect Omega who had been making such progress was pacing.

"Claire, look at me." Shepherd caught her arm to put an end to her anxious behavior.

Chewing her cuticle, concerned green eyes met his.

"I would not allow you to be anywhere where I did not know you were perfectly safe. Remember that when you have your tantrum after I leave."

9

High-handed, unconcerned with the liberties he took… Shepherd had made his move. Claire saw that now, frustrated that clarity only struck in the wake of his ploys. He wanted her angry, mentioned her impending *tantrum* especially so she might snarl in indignation.

An angry Claire was not an anxious Claire. And she was angry.

Very angry now that it all sank in.

It was more than just the mess he had made of her nest… again. It was a never-ending pull.

He wanted a tantrum so that she would perform per his strategy, yet he was the one who'd left feathers everywhere. Nests were sacred to Omegas, they were art. Alphas were to admire them and relish the efforts of their mates.

In Thólos, he had respected her nest, encouraged it.

Invaded on his whim. Now, they were taken for granted in his pursuit to… what? Annoy her?

His seed flowed down her thighs, a slippery reminder that he had only just fucked her and left. Downy feathers were in her hair, sticking to the mess as it ran down her legs. It would take an army of people to clean this room in the two hours she would sit and practice Greth's Spanish.

Which would mean strangers near her most sacred space. Many strangers. Their scents would stain the air, a condition no Omega would appreciate.

So she would have to do it herself. Which, of course, he *knew* she would do.

Which was another reason it was obvious he had made the mess on purpose. Frustrations surging, she reached for her COMscreen and dialed her mate. He answered immediately.

"If you wanted to see a movie, you could have just said, 'Claire, I want to see a movie about a baker.' You didn't need to destroy my house!"

There was no visual, but she could hear the smirk in his reply. "You would have declined the invitation."

"I am so angry with you right now." And she was growing more angry by the moment. "Why can't you just be normal?"

No emotion layered his reply. "Watching a film is normal, little one."

"You planned this whole thing from the beginning. This was all one big setup!"

"*Victorious warriors win first and then go to war, while*

defeated warriors go to war first and then seek to win.' You should spend more time studying your favorite philosopher if you want to outwit me, Mrs. O'Donnell."

One hand held the screen, the other tore at her hair. "The fact that you see our marriage as a war tells me that you need to be the one talking to Dr. Osin, not me."

"I'm at war with your neurosis, Claire O'Donnell." Utterly calm, as if he had prepared his answers to her anger weeks ahead of time, he said, "You reek of fear at the thought of leaving our home. You refuse the company of others. Your self-imposed solitude is over. I am ordering you to make a friend."

"You are completely insane!"

"You claimed I am tense lately. Perhaps I would be less tense if my mate were more well."

Her feelings stung at the barb, Claire aware that even if his COM did not show a visual, he was absolutely watching her. That he saw how her lip shook before she could stop it. "I am not one of your Followers. You don't get to order me to do anything."

Darkness promising so many things purred over the line. "Then I shall continue to outwit you. Have fun cleaning up the feathers. I love you, and I will see you at dusk."

The connection terminated.

Fuming, Claire looked around the wreckage of their bedroom and screamed. Hating that she knew he was still watching her. That he would be watching her all day.

"Wow." Maryanne leaned back in her chair, baffled and grossed out. Also not entirely sure it would be a good idea to tell Shepherd he had a small white feather in his hair. "You guys sound so *normal*."

Tucking away his COMscreen, Shepherd poured such a look on Maryanne that her moxy fled.

Throwing her hands up, she said, "I know you ordered me not to speak, but she's not on the line anymore. And it's strange, you know? I have not heard my best friend's voice in over a year." Unsure why she had a death wish, Maryanne added, "Why doesn't she have friends? Claire was always popular. A total teacher's pet too. Everyone loves Claire, they always have."

"If you do not report on Jules in the next ten seconds, I will break your neck and replace you."

Rolling her eyes, Maryanne flicked the screen that held a breakdown of her daily report, including segments of video footage for Shepherd to absorb.

"As you can see, Jules remains in a cell. He receives two meals a day, which he refuses to eat. Despite standard intimidation and bribery, he has also refused to interact with his visitors: identified as Commodore Jacques Bernard and Ancil Vox, Head of Bernard Dome Security—which was ridiculously easy to infiltrate. Whoever is supervising their communications network, they are not reacting to my invasion as a *professional* would. I don't think they even know

I'm there. I think it's also relevant to note that Jules has not signaled."

His cold "You have access to everything?" was not the gold star she felt she earned.

Maryanne should have known better than to expect Shepherd to offer praise for a job well done. "So far. Including the Commodore's bedchambers. Those videos will give you nightmares."

Crossing his arms in a way that stretched his suit coat, Shepherd studied the monitors. "Tell me about the woman."

"The scarred Omega? Her name's Brenya Perin, the new mate of Commodore Bernard. As noted in previous reports, most surveillance of them are… of a sexual nature."

"Show me."

Several monitors filled with recorded examples of the Omega heaving under her Alpha. In all of them, she appeared unresponsive—until the bloom of Alpha coercion manipulated her physiology into an empty shell that stopped resisting and climaxed from the pressure of a knot.

To be honest, Maryanne found it… disturbingly familiar.

Years ago, Claire had come to Maryanne in such a state. Battered, frightened, but there was a clear difference between the two Omegas. Claire had refused surrender. Brenya Perin was the embodiment of defeat.

Glancing at her boss from the corner of her eye, Maryanne knew Shepherd saw it too. His jaw ticking as his unwavering stare catalogued everything.

"Do you want to know what I think, Shepherd?"

Eyes that could see right down to her rotten soul turned

from the screen and weighed her down with one unbroken glare.

Her throat bobbed in a swallow, the icy fingers of impending death scratching at her spine. "I think you need to watch this."

Flicking the controls, the screens went black, the grunts and sounds of sex snuffed out. All that was left was a single monitor offering a cheery, sun-drenched nursery.

"The runtime is one hour, five minutes, and twenty-seven seconds." Glancing back at the Alpha monstrosity, Maryanne added, "You might want to take a seat."

Ignoring her offer, Shepherd stood through the entire recording of Brenya Perin having tea with Security Advisor Ancil Vox's first wife. Maryanne had already watched the video three times, making notations on each timestamped twitch, focusing less on the depressing exchange of two sad women and more on the physical oddness.

"Brenya Perin isn't neurotypical. She cannot understand nuance or subtlety. She can hardly interact in this social situation without mimicking her hostess. Yet she is counting every single object in the room, unaware that she is doing it." Those words had already been in her report, but reading an opinion versus viewing it for oneself? "She sees everything and notices nothing."

Shepherd, it would seem, had come to the same conclusion. "She's a genius."

"Annette confronts Brenya for *running*. The ship your Followers monitored flying toward Thólos three days ago? I think Brenya stole it. That woman piloted a craft with no training, somehow managed to get outside the Dome, was apprehended halfway to Thólos, and was returned mated to the Commodore. Just look at her. She's battered he bit her *twice*. The mangled claiming mark on her neck was still bleeding badly enough to leave a decent stain on her dress."

There was no agreement or negation from Shepherd. He simply waited for Maryanne to continue her report.

"Jules was imprisoned because of her escape. He's refusing to eat, meanwhile these women are discussing honey and Beta rations." There was no point in beating around the bush, so Maryanne just admitted she didn't understand what that meant. "What are Beta rations?"

Shocking the fuck out of her, he actually explained. "Outside of the ruling class, the citizens of Bernard Dome are fed pharmaceuticals from birth to keep them complacent and obedient. That is why Jules is choosing to starve."

Okay, since they were having a heart-to-heart, she figured she'd do it thoroughly. "Why not just send him home? If he dies, they must know you will end them all. You're not subtle in your threats, Shepherd."

"Give me a close up of Ms. Perin's bite marks."

"Done." That had all been prepared, needed only a flick of a key to display the poor girl's shoulder and neck. "See? He practically ripped her throat in half."

"I want a full dossier prepared on Brenya Perin. I want to know everything about that female."

"I've already looked." Maryanne scrambled to change the screens to the little data she'd scrounged up. "They must have scrubbed her file from the census. The only reason I know her full name is because it is mentioned in conversation."

"You have observed her for days, so answer this. Would Claire feel an affinity for this Omega?"

Maryanne had to snort at that. "Oh Gods, yes, Claire would go full savior mode at one glance of this socially awkward weirdo."

"I would suggest you speak more kindly of Jules' mate."

It had to be a joke. It had to be! After all, Maryanne was cackling at the idea of Jules with a woman. Not only that. "Jules is a Beta."

Shepherd's silence was heavy with annoyance and something that almost tasted like grief.

Why on earth Maryanne felt the need to assure him, she didn't know. "Betas cannot pair-bond. After the Commodore gets his panties out of a twist, they will send him home."

But Shepherd just kept staring at her.

Stuttering, Maryanne said, "It's... it's not possible."

"Had you spent your time in the Undercroft gathering wisdom, listening to the stories of the men suffering, instead of pissing yourself every time someone screamed, you would have learned that there were a multitude of sordid reasons a man was disposed of instead of murdered."

The very concept was extremely upsetting, and Maryanne didn't quite understand why. "Betas cannot initiate pair-bonds. It's basic biology."

"His name was Keriman. There was another called Wess. Two men with the same tale. Two men who had never met one another, Keriman long dead before Wess was thrown into the dark. Both Alpha, both having claimed they had been used by powerful Betas who *coveted* and were tricked into sharing their bond. Their new mates were stolen, and each man was thrown into the Undercroft to suffer until they went mad from separation."

"I checked the registries after Thólos fell. The Beta named by Keriman married an Omega. She had been institutionalized and died within a year of Keriman's incarceration. The Omega Wess claimed to have bonded to, a Beta Senator, had set herself on fire… one year after he had been thrown underground."

"If such a thing were possible, people would know. Everyone would know!"

Except they wouldn't. No Alpha would submit to such a thing willingly. Nor would powerful Betas be allowed to retain a taboo bond should their Alpha brethren discover what they had done.

Standing tall, Shepherd gave his final order of the day. "Brenya Perin. You will find the traces of her erased registry. I want to know everything."

The strangest wave of sadness came over her. "If it's true, Jules won't ever be able to come home."

The man had already begun merging with the shadows, yet he hesitated for a simple moment. And that was confirmation enough.

10

Her husband was a total bastard.

Every feather had been picked from the floor by hand, collected in a bin to be repurposed. Claire's morning spent on her hands and knees chasing fluff as it shifted around the room each time she moved.

At midday, Dr. Osin invaded—as the psychiatrist did any time Claire attempted to miss a session—and she found the Omega still plucking feathers, one at a time, from the carpet.

"You were to meet with me at two." Ever the Alpha, the no-nonsense statement fell without sympathy for the mess.

Wiping her hair from her sweaty forehead, Claire sat back on her heels and let out a breath. Unsure if she was more annoyed by the task at hand or the interruption, she cut a glare over her shoulder. "Yeah, well, Shepherd decided to be Shepherd."

Still standing on the threshold of the room, Dr. Osin

sniffed the air. "It smells as if you recently mated."

"He calls it *making love*." Sarcasm thick, Claire reached for another feather. "Making love as he destroys my nests and disregards my feelings."

"The only thing Shepherd regards *is* your feelings. Therefore, one might assume your assumption is incorrect."

Tossing her hair and turning back to her work, Claire gave the Alpha her back. "I am not in the mood for your Shepherd ass-kissing propaganda today. Either help me clean up this mess or leave."

"I have brought lunch. Your mess can wait until after you have eaten. Shepherd informed me that you had forgotten. He also informed me your breakfast was cut short."

Of course he was checking in on her, the man couldn't seem to go a day without stalking his wife in every possible way. "Cut short is one way to phrase it. Or one might say I made a reasonable request, was manhandled, tossed into my nest, and fucked so hard I'm sore. Then in a show of complete insanity, he tore my favorite pillow in half and scattered feathers that I now have the honor of cleaning up."

Unmoved by the agitation of the Omega, Dr. Osin said, "We were discussing your eating habits. We'll save your sex life for another session."

Three more feathers gathered, Claire brushed off the old woman's usual abruptness. "I didn't forget lunch. I prefer not to eat when I'm anxious."

As if anything Dr. Osin might offer could possibly tempt her, the Follower said, "I brought a popular local dish from the Dome's best Omega restaurant."

Picking another feather from the rug, Claire swiveled to her hip, staring down the intruder again as she spun the feather between her thumb and fingers. "Greth has Omega restaurants?"

Unabashedly observing the state of her charge, the old woman nodded. "Omegas are plentiful in this Dome and catered to. Spoiled. My mate would have swanned around and smirked at me quite a bit had he seen the life here. You'd know that if you ever went outside these grounds."

The dig wasn't missed, but it also wasn't effective.

Even if she were willing to venture into the city, Claire would not step anywhere near a public Omega space. The very idea was ludicrous. Alphas would lurk. Omegas would be harassed, stalked home, cornered, taken. Heaven only knew how Shepherd would react if someone so much as whistled in her general direction.

Furthermore, there was a reason Omegas didn't have public places. There was a reason that being Omega meant to either adapt to the Beta population or avoid Alphas unless one desired a pair-bond. Even mated Omegas kept their heads down if they were smart. They shopped for groceries in the daylight, most likely with a family escort. They didn't tour the promenade alone or sip coffee in the breeze.

Not unless they lived as Claire had lived. Not unless no one knew they were Omega.

"What are you thinking, Claire?"

Pressing up from the ground, she brushed a few straggling feathers from her skirt. "I'm thinking it sounds too good to be true. Therefore, it's a ploy. Wise Omegas only congregate in private, in secret. It's sacred. I don't believe there is such a thing as an Omega restaurant unless it's managed by Alphas trying to lure in easy prey."

"If you'd bothered to read the chapters I prepared for you on the local population, Mrs. O'Donnell, then you would know that there are more Omegas per capita than Alphas in Greth. They outnumber their matching dynamic. Competition for mates is fierce. Omegas walk freely, dress provocatively—"

"Enough." Claire put up her hands to end the madness. "I don't have any interest in discussing this topic. Grethentine Omegas can do what they want, but I am Thólosen, and we don't speak about our dynamic with Alphas."

Cocking her head, Dr. Osin said, "You not talking about Omegas is the reason they are all dead back in Thólos and not living a good life here."

Her fingers curled into fists, Claire clenching her jaw so hard it ached. "Shepherd really did send you with the mission to piss me off today."

Leaning against the door, Dr. Osin crossed her arms over her chest. "You think more clearly when you're angry. No point in denying it."

Snarling, Claire showed teeth. "Then I am clearly telling you to go fuck yourself. I don't want your Omega fancy food. I'll make my own fucking lunch when I fucking feel like it."

"How long has it been since you've thought about the Omegas you *saved* back in Thólos? Nona, wasn't that the name of the one you were close to? The murderess?"

Claire's blood went ice-cold, her eyes narrowing. "I think you need to leave now."

Instead, the doctor took another step inside Claire's room. "Isn't this where you try to explain? Don't you want to tell me about the Omega sanctuary and how the survivors gathered up all the broken women? Didn't they keep them like caged birds in a pretty building that won't have power by the end of the year? Did they drug them like they drugged you? What happens when the rest of the survivors realize that all the pretty Omegas live in luxury while they all suffer in the Undercroft? Infected with Da'rin and eating mold. A gruesome end awaits those Omegas because of you."

Stalking right up to the vicious Dr. Osin, Claire snarled, "I refuse to bear the blame for what Followers did to Thólos. I will *NOT* feel guilt for doing the right thing and keeping good women away from Shepherd's men!" Red-faced, raging, she stuck a finger in the old woman's face and screamed, "We chose what we wanted. We all did. Not one of us chose you!"

Batting away the finger Claire had put in her face, Dr. Osin shrugged. "And now all your friends are dead, stranded, mated, or missing. And you are so frightened of connecting with anyone that you are terrified to attend a social setting. What might you see when you get there? Who are you going to want to save with your misguided hero complex?"

She had gone past agitation, and known moments of rage, and now... *now*, Claire was still as a viper ready to strike. "You want me to say what we all already know. I am aware that to Shepherd, when it comes to his mate's friends, a person has the same worth as the pillow he tore apart this morning. Nothing but a tool he could use to make a point or destroy at will. What point is there in having a friend that he will threaten and terrify? I will not allow him to use my affections to force me to do things against my judgment."

"Your judgment is flawed."

"And you are a sycophant drunk on the punch. Shepherd is not a God. I love him as a man, but I want nothing to do with his cult."

"I am hearing a whole lot of excuses for 'I'm scared to go outside because I am a fragile Omega who can't handle her mate.'"

"Handle Shepherd?" Claire actually laughed. And then she laughed some more. "How many times has he threatened your life specifically in relation to me?"

Dr. Osin did not hesitate to answer. "Five."

Which was both hilarious and completely insane! "And you say it as if it were normal."

"It is normal. Shepherd is a king, responsible for the well-being of an entire Dome, caring for his recovering, difficult Omega, and beholden to his Followers—who put their lives and the lives of their families at risk so all of us might live free. Shepherd has the responsibility of the entire world upon his shoulders. And you—pretending there is no work to be done—you think a fancy nest will solve his problems? You add to his burden, Claire O'Donnell, by refusing to be the strong, worthy mate an Alpha of his stature needs at his side."

Oh... Dr. Osin was going to get it.

"When I look at you, all prim and dressed in black, do you know what I see?" There was no backing down from such an insult, Claire moving closer so that unless Dr. Osin wanted to be brushed with the scent of furious Omega, the old woman had to step back. And then she had to step back again as Claire continued to sneer and pursue. "I see bodies hanging from trees. I smell corpses piled up on causeways. I hear children crying for their parents. I taste rot in my mouth. Go live free in Shepherd's *new world*. I know my sins, and I will not repeat them. I will not inflict him on anyone else. I will stay here, and the Dome will be a safer place for everyone."

Having backed the Alpha female to the door of her home, Claire snarled, "Now, get out!"

It was the first time Claire had seen an Alpha look even slightly intimidated by an Omega, and it felt good to cow the old bitch. It felt better to slam the door in her face.

When her COMscreen began to instantly ring, Claire lifted it up over her head and slammed it down on the floor, pleased at how broken bits of it scattered. Then she went back to her bedroom and continued cleaning up the feathers.

No new nest was prepared. Shepherd could sleep like a Beta for all she cared.

∼

HE ARRIVED AT DUSK, just as he said he would. A new COMscreen in his hand for his mate. Claire was in her garden, sitting in the very nook where she had wanted to host a romantic moment for them. Still angry, watching the Alpha approach, hurt obvious in her tense body language and sullen stare.

Setting the COMscreen on the wrought iron table between them, he lowered his bulk into the adjoining chair. "You are right to believe that I would use any personal attachments you formed against your wishes, if I believed it was in your best interest. But consider, our situation in Thólos was dire. You consistently placed yourself in danger. You tried to kill yourself, little one." Gravity weighed down his voice, it weighed down the man. "And you would have continued walking forward on that ice had I not held the safety of your friends over you."

Claire couldn't deny any of it. Couldn't even summon an argument to counter.

Gray eyes held hers, as Shepherd softly added, "I kept my word, Claire."

Wiping her cheek with the back of her hand, Claire said, "I know. Dr. Osin kindly reminded me that the Omegas trapped and dying in Thólos are thanks to my opposition to your regime."

"That is not what I am referring to." His fingers drummed the table, as if the Alpha debated reaching for her hand or giving Claire her space. "Maryanne is alive. She is in Greth. And she will remain alive, because that is what I promised you."

Expression stunned, Claire stumbled over her words. "Why… wasn't I—"

"You know why." He did reach for her fingers then,

gentle as he placed his hand atop hers. "The mere mention of Thólos in those first months sent you into a dangerous psychosis. You've come so far, little one. Your spark, I can see it inside you. The same fierce flame that walked into the dark Citadel to face down her tormentor."

The nervous question came from an anxious woman. One who feared the worst. "How is she?"

"You would be surprised to see how well she's doing. Structure and discipline have slowly turned a lackluster, selfish monster into—"

"—a Follower." The word tasted like mud.

Shepherd blinked but didn't respond.

The link felt so strained, so out of harmony, that Claire unconsciously pulled her hand from his and placed it where her sternum ached. "I want to see her."

"Maryanne must serve five more years of her sentence. The time is well-spent and engaging. It employs her skillset while she monitors communication feeds and the people of this Dome. The lock on her door is simple, she could have escaped into the city at any time. Yet she has chosen to stay. Meanwhile, her work has kept many good people, including yourself, safe. It has kept Greth at peace during the transition of leadership."

Rubbing her chest all the harder, Claire said with more force, "I want to see her."

Turning his hand over and offering his palm, he motioned with a cock of his head for her to take it. Claire hesitated. She hesitated, looking down at his waiting hand, frowning. But she did tentatively reach forward and lay her fingers on his.

Only to hear him deny her.

"No." Trapping her by his grip, Shepherd softly repeated the word. "No."

Lip curled in disgust, the Omega grumbled, "You are going to force me to go see your film in exchange for Maryanne."

"Little one, if she is ever going to reach her potential, Maryanne needs a structured life right now that doesn't involve you. I give you my word we will revisit this when her sentence is served, but for now, you must leave her be. More importantly, she cannot be distracted from her current task, as it involves the safety of another person you care about."

"You're in danger?" Her hackles went up, Claire glancing around the courtyard as if some villain might rush forward and harm her mate.

"Jules was sent on a diplomatic mission to a Dome in Europe called Bernard. There has been an incident. Maryanne is working day and night to assure he survives it."

The bottom dropped out from under her, Claire sucking in a breath as she realized just why the pair-bond hurt so much in that moment. Shepherd was... he was melancholy. Not that he would ever show it, but grief was all around him. And she had added to it that day.

Even if her reasons were sound, it was as Dr. Osin said. She was a burden on a man already weighed down with so much. So she placed her other hand atop where theirs were joined, and said, "Tell me what happened."

He gave her fingers a squeeze, gray eyes tracking to where his Omega offered comfort despite her indignation.

"There isn't enough information yet to state a hypothesis as fact. But I will say, if my suspicion is correct, he will never return to Greth."

What was a girl to say to a mass-murdering tyrant who lost what might be the closest he would ever have to a friend? "I am sorry, Shepherd."

In a very human gesture, the man rubbed his face, closing his eyes as he drew in a deep breath. When he pinched the bridge of his nose and sighed, Claire grew unnerved.

Only once had she seen Shepherd emote on this level, the night he handed her to another Alpha so she might be transported safely away from him. The night he was going to give his life for her and their son.

"Shepherd, whatever you're thinking, don't do it."

His lashes parted, gray eyes liquid—as if they stung. "I'm thinking that Collin would have celebrated his second birthday this month."

A pained sound hitched in Claire's throat, her heart splitting right down the middle.

But it was as if the Alpha didn't see her grief at the mention of their dead son, he was too wrapped up in his own. "Every day, I watch Followers' families thrive. I watch them play with their children. *And I envy them.* They *live,* and I cannot even entice my perfect Omega, my beautiful wife, to attend a film with me. I have never known normal, Claire O'Donnell. And I grasp that you will punish me for the rest of our lives for my sins. The irony is not lost."

With that, he left her in the garden alone. Entering their home as if he desired to be alone.

11

BERNARD DOME

Wiping his lips on a snowy-white napkin, Jacques set starched fabric to the matching tablecloth. Fingers lingering over the formality, the Alpha male pensive, he said, "Brenya, I know it must appear to you that these complications are insurmountable, but I assure you, they are not."

Brenya spun a forkful of Pâtes d'Alsace on her spoon, just as she had seen Jacques demonstrate when the pasta course arrived. The action was... soothing. The twist of the wrist, the mechanical requirement to use two utensils. Like tools fine tuning a sprog.

Yet somewhat exacerbating.

Before reassignment to Central, Brenya had never participated in a meal that required more than one utensil.

The little tools in her hand, solid gold and weightier than the sporks supplied to the masses, offered a semblance of what she missed. At least, she had slowly come to grasp that she could simulate the fine detail work of her true vocation in pointless everyday exercises.

Work within the confines of your station and situation.

The fork, for example: gold was soft, malleable at low temperatures, a poor choice for any tool, but an excellent choice for improvising in a pinch. That was fascinating, in a sense. Each tine might be reworked to create something beyond a food stabbing device. The curve-shaped length of the utensil was similar to that of a lever. She could pry open generally anything that didn't require much force.

With that fork and a strategy, she could dissect Jacques' bedroom in a day. Considering that he always left the dinner course out on the patio setting where he preferred they share their evening meal, she had access to two forks. Two knives. Two spoons.

Gold conducted electricity extremely well. This sample in her hand wasted on something used for food. Had she the ability to draw out the metal, enough wire could be created to build... well... lots of things.

Outside of her specific assignment, improvising was frowned upon in Beta Sector, yet she had a knack for imagining what might be. Not that she had ever told any of her sisters or friends. Brenya saved such things for work. Like the time during an emergency *descent* when she had saved an entire loose panel from crashing down the Dome. Had it fully broken free, the weighty thing would have done catastrophic damage. Yet while others braced against the glass by her side, Brenya used her suction grip bars as if they had been intended to fortify two panels and not bear her weight.

Which was strictly forbidden when making the climb.

Protocol, focus, process, acceptance.

There had been no fanfare when the panel was saved. The highest praise she received for thinking on her feet had been the utter lack of mention of her breach of procedure. There had been no write up.

George had even smiled at her when they were alone to talk over the daily status report.

How strange it was not having him in her ear, the pair of them working as one to assure the comfort and safety of all.

But Brenya had breathed outside air, become Omega, harmed him by association, and had no one to share such thoughts with anymore.

It would have been better if that panel had fallen and left growing cracks all the way down the Dome. At least then, the city would know that the air outside smelled sweet, that the virus had moved on. That they could go outside and see butterflies. That paranoia was unnecessary, and a new life could begin.

The abandoned cities could be reclaimed by those with the drive to find what the world offered.

Clearing his throat, Jacques tried again to solicit her attention. "It has been four days, *mon chou*, since your tea with Annette. You have had nothing to say on the topic."

Responding automatically, Brenya continued to swirl a fresh bite for a stomach that starved no matter how much it ate. "The tea was a blend of ginger, turmeric, and rosehip.

Honey was added. Something of a Centrist tradition to acknowledge that Alpha mates are cruel."

The male settled both of his hands upon the small table they shared, leaning forward, before he asked, "You believe I am cruel?"

"I have no perspective to make such a judgment. Ancil is the only other male in Central I have seen outside of the state dinner in which Annette was poisoned with Beta rations. I would need more than two variables to make a reasonable assessment." Honey eyes looked up from her work trying to gather slippery bits of carbohydrates covered in sauce to abstractly consider the Alpha watching her. "Then there is the outlying concern. If you lived in Beta sector, you would have been put to death the day you raped me in the alley."

"*Brenya.*" It was not her first warning of the day.

The noodles were waiting on her spoon, right there. Eating when she was so hungry seemed more relevant than conversation. After all, the Alpha had a history of forgetting she was a living thing that required water, air, and sustenance. "Have I done something wrong?"

"*Mon chou....*" Lifting his glass, ice tinkling against the crystal, Jacques sipped, staring at her over the rim.

If he was going to leave things unspoken, she was going to eat. The tiny nest of pasta went into her mouth, chewed in fascination of the strange texture. After a swallow, she immediately began to prepare another bite.

"You seem unusually hungry."

It might have been the first relevant comment the Alpha had made that evening. Relevant enough that she looked up from her dwindling plate and shifted a modicum of her attention from thoughts of gold forks to the symmetry of his face.

When they were alone, Jacques wore his hair loose, blond waves cascading over broad shoulders. Brenya was very familiar with the procedure of unweaving the braid and setting it loose, that being one of the duties he outlined would be hers as his mate. He'd purr and groan as she worked through those locks, her fingers systematically working through the procedure to the exact count of sixty seconds. When it was done, she would fellate him before he might decide to seek other indulgences. Just as Annette had taught her.

Sprawled in his chair, she would begin counting, following his requests, ignoring how often he made her gag or how much her jaw might ache. And where her fingers had been in his hair, his were now tangled in hers, the Alpha moving her to whatever rhythm he favored.

It was a race to excite him enough he might come down her throat and save her from another mounting. His changing moods made it difficult to keep up with the uncontrolled thing he became when aroused. Desperation led her to suck harder, move faster, drool everywhere so he might finish and leave her alone.

At least for an hour while he smirked in his chair and watched her stare out the window. That was if he didn't drag her to his lap for a long kiss and hold her there until he was done doing whatever it was he thought to accomplish by keeping her tucked under his chin.

Two of the last four days, she had either overperformed in

this act or underperformed, both times ending up stuffed full of cock and knotted by a rutting male who bruised where he gripped. Her back to his damp chest, he would place his hot palm where his seed left her belly distended and purr. The longer the knot, the more his fingers might slip down to toy with the sensitive flesh between her legs, compelling another orgasm he timed with his next gush.

The slosh of what he left inside her body, what was plugged by his bulbous, pulsating knot. Brenya both knew relief when his member shrank enough to set the torrent free, and disgust from the way his fluids would flood over her thighs.

It was *so much*.

A pool of Alpha sperm. And for some reason, it seemed as if each time she braced for his pleasure, he produced more.

He'd want her to lay in that cooling sticky mess, touching and rumbling, saying things she ignored. He'd hold her there despite all her aches and the sting between her legs, despite the scratches and the weeping bites that seemed to bleed every time he put his hands on her with a sexual intent.

One day. All she wanted was *one day* without some part of his body inside some part of hers.

Heaven help her if she winced at any of his handling, because that meant a session with the pliarator.

As if any machine might stretch her enough that his member would ever fit without pain.

"You will struggle to deliver children, petite as you are," Jacques had murmured, manipulating the pliarator as she writhed. "It is a pity we will have to scar your beautiful skin to get them out."

The idea of baring a child in the Centrist fashion—one that would be exposed to this man—led to a reaction that ignored logic and ended in disaster. Instead of struggling against the pliarator, she lifted a leg and kicked him right in the chest. The machine slipped from her channel, the man was displaced long enough for her to escape that gross puddle and run out of the bed.

Right into the bathroom.

Where she locked the door as if that might actually keep him out.

He ripped it off the hinges, wood splintering as if it took little effort.

Naked, slimy, cornered, thin arms around her middle, and trying to hide behind her hair, Brenya shrank.

"You won't even be awake for the procedure, Brenya. There is no reason to react in such a way. Your penchant for violence and threats is…." He took her arm, dragging her from the room. It was hard to keep up with his stride, her legs still shaking from the pliarator effect on her nerves.

He never finished his statement, spinning her about until the mattress hit her belly and her legs dangled to the floor.

She heard the clicks and knew what it meant. He was resetting the machine, altering the program, before that horrible thing might find a new home.

Crying through it all, she bore the burning anal stretch, hiccupping when the Alpha allowed the machine to simulate a knot that must have stretched her until her burning ring was bloodless and white.

The hands stroking her back and the unwelcome platitudes did nothing to ease even a moment of it. Brenya couldn't even reach out to that dangerous void of the other person who was somehow there and somehow not.

When the cycle was finished and her throat was raw from sobbing, he removed the things, showing her that it bore no trace of blood. Chastising her for her lack of trust and overreaction.

That was to be her punishment when she needed correction, and also a boon. She would soon be able to take him up her ass in the way men sometimes preferred. And soon, it would give her only pleasure. Just as obedience would.

If she would only behave, he would say, she would learn that all he did was for her pleasure.

And she had wiped her nose, slinking off the bed. Staring at the floor, she nodded.

That was why there was a soft pillow atop her chair at their shared dinner.

He tried to chat with her as if another punishment had never happened. Already, he assured her she was utterly forgiven.

After she had calmed and accepted the endless throbbing soreness of being a female Omega, Brenya was able to slip back into the emotionless space of a Beta who had a Rebecca.

The Alpha across from her increased the volume of his

purr as if pleased at her perusal, and stated for the second time, "I said, you seem unusually hungry."

"Yes. I am very hungry."

The demeanor of the man before her went from preening to assessing. "Yet you have eaten enough for a grown Alpha."

That was true, and her belly did ache for it. But what did that matter? She hurt everywhere.

"Are you in pain?"

It's not like he couldn't see the bruises, the bite marks. It's not like he had not been the person to place the pillow she was sitting upon because her labia and anus were stinging and swollen. So she didn't answer. The question had to be a rhetorical one.

Heavy male fingers trilled over the tabletop, Jacques' voice terse. "Specifically in regards to your digestion. Are you in pain?"

Fork stabbed noodles and carried them to the waiting spoon so she might spin another bite.

Bringing his fist under his chin, the Alpha narrowed his eyes and leaned his weight forward. "You are ordered to tell me when you are uncomfortable."

That was simple enough. "I am uncomfortable."

Sighing, he threw his weight back into his chair, hand to the air as if beseeching the Gods for help. "Brenya, please try."

More pasta was chewed, swallowed, to land in a distended belly that ached with emptiness. "I don't understand what answer you want me to give you. You know I am in pain."

"If you wish to discuss what happened earlier, then there is no answer required. The harder I fuck you, the closer you grow to accepting your place as my mate. When I am gentle, you are restless, lying under me with your eyes closed and your body limp. When I am rough, you engage."

"You want me to fight back because I no longer say no when you mount me?" There were so many flaws in that statement, so much ugliness to it, that her stomach roiled and all the noodles were about to come up.

"You don't touch me, *mon chou*."

That was untrue. "I stimulate your erection with my hands in the exact way you taught me to. I use my mouth and tongue to fulfill the commands given as you move my head. I swallow."

"What if I were to organize an event where you could watch an Alpha and Omega mate properly? Is that what you need to see to understand that you are more to me than the pretty pussy I knot? Your place is in the moment, seeking pleasure from your mate instead of tolerating."

"At lunch, your coat had exactly twenty-four buttons. Now, you wear a coat with seven. Why are you wearing a different coat?" Why did Centrist do anything the way they did?

The male sighed. "Because it is dinner, Brenya. And that's how things are done."

And of course, that made no sense to her. "And if I touch

you when you mount me, you'll make it hurt less? Because that is how things are done?"

The man looked as if her words cut him, as if she were the one causing him pain. "You are tormenting me with your indifference."

12

Considering the subject matter, a straightforward approach would serve better than manipulation. After all, the Commodore had tried the simplicity of allowing things to run their course, offering dignity to a man who deserved none. It would have been a simple thing for Jules Havel to eat his meals, the Beta mellowing after digesting the proper dosage for a male of his size and strength. The secondary buffer—beyond the joint pair-bond—necessary.

The entire fate of Bernard Dome was at stake—not to mention the safety of Jacques' precious mate.

And though he would prefer the ease of simply killing the man, Jules needed to be alive and well to serve his function. Protecting Brenya, and therefore all of his people, from Chancellor Shepherd's threat of unleashing the virus.

But these exchanges were growing tiresome.

Or, lack of exchange, for a better word.

With Brenya back in their nest, knowing she slept fitfully without him, Jacques had rushed dressing to confront a burden, grabbing a midday coat instead of an evening jacket. The enlightening dinner he had just shared with his mate having changed everything regarding forward momentum in retaining her happiness.

It had made Jacques leave the peace of his bed to deal with a fiend where they would not be overheard by a sweetly chiming Omega soul.

Entering the viewing area outside the cell of his new rabid dog, Jacques adjusted his cuff. The male within undeserving of his full attention, considering his behavior. "Ambassador Havel, did you know there are no prisons in Bernard Dome? Until your arrival, they were unnecessary."

The man behind the clear amorphous metal did not so much as turn his head to acknowledge that the Commodore had paid him yet another personal visit.

Jules Havel, mercenary and madman, simply sat on the floor and stared at the bleak, gray wall before him. His behavior predictable, boring even.

"I ordered this installation converted the night I agreed to Chancellor Shepherd's trade. Previously, this storage room was stocked with racks of aging red wines. As you must have noticed, Ambassador, the walls are solid—a meter of cement to maintain the optimum temperature with little intervention of electricity. Unfortunately, there is no plumbing, hence the bucket. A short-term solution should a complicated situation arise."

And a complication had arisen, Jacques grateful for his foresight. Which was why he was Commodore and all who contested his rule were dead.

"Ambassador Havel, this was never intended to be your long-term *home*." Yet it had been the perfect kennel for a foreign threat. "Merely a place of transition and transformation. Yet it seems you wish to stay."

The cuff of Jacques' fresh shirt was properly adjusted, the Alpha moved to correct the other sleeve. "You see, in Bernard Dome, on the rare occurrence of criminal behavior, the instigator is instantly euthanized—a humane process that has worked for centuries and led to a peaceful population. My city, it is a treasure of culture and refinement in this empty world. The perfect civilization: ordered, organized, maintained, and cultivated. Paradise at the price of a steady decline in the Omega population… until there were none to be found. Being Beta, you cannot imagine what it is like to be an Alpha missing his other half and living in a world where it will never appear."

Just like every other encounter the males had shared since they both fucked an Estrous-high Brenya Perin into the perfection of a three-way pair-bond, Jules Havel refused to acknowledge his presence.

But that did not matter. The ancient fables were correct, and the Beta was fully bound.

"Brenya was in a room similar to this one for days after an accident almost took her from me forever. Quarantined after exposure when she fell down the side of the Dome and shattered her helmet. That is why the wound on her face healed so poorly. She had no medical care. I love that scar, the perfect reminder of the miracle that brought my Omega to me. It is a symbol of what must be done to weed out females who might potentially find their own miracle in monitored seclusion. Fifteen more Omegas have been discovered with this method in the last seven days. A percentage of the population that will bring so many hope and has freed me from any further association with Greth Dome, Chancellor Shepherd, or unenlightened foreigners."

Sleeves perfected, Jacques finally ran his attention over the silent Beta and let out a sigh. "You have been given a great gift despite your threats to my people. Freedom from the tyranny of your past, an opportunity to contribute to greatness. A greater gift still in knowing a bond with a pure-hearted Omega. Considering the taboo even in mythology, not one in a billion Betas has ever known such a thing."

At last, Jules, brown hair falling into blue eyes of unnatural brightness, deigned to turn his head.

Progress. So, Jacques got to the point. "You are making her sick by refusing to eat."

His prisoner did not so much as blink. He just stared in the eerie way of the dangerous and the evil.

"I have been reasonable with you, Jules Havel. I invited you into my home, extending goodwill. Furthermore, I have kept to Chancellor Shepherd's request that Bernard Dome not interfere with Thólos." As if Jacques would waste his people's resources on a failed civilization that had birthed the very men who had turned and eaten it.

No intonation, no apparent interest in negotiation, Jules replied, "I won't swallow anything that I have not seen Brenya Perin taste first."

With a scoff, Jacques smirked. "I will not expose my mate to you."

Those piercing eyes burned, saying in their unwavering stare that Jacques had fully exposed the female to him. That there was no part of her that he had not seen, no sexual act that had not been performed before him. That he had fucked her too. "Continue to attempt to feed me Beta rations, and she won't be your mate for long."

Enough of this.

"I saw the way you looked at her—at the state dinner, on your ship." Jacques' nostrils flared, his ire rising at the audacity of the cretin who had nothing to barter with. "How you salivated watching me claim the female who is *mine*. You even have my sympathy. One look and I wanted the strange girl too. Yet, I allowed you to taste her once... so that she could be safe from you forever. You will not enjoy her again. That will be your burden in exchange for your survival."

As if he might see her through the ceiling, Jules turned his gaze upward. "The Omega told me why she stole my ship. Candid to a fault in her desperation to be free of you. I felt her grief to wake bonded to a male who disgusts her. Ever since, she has been calling to me, unknowing what she does. The female gets a little closer every day. A little more trusting. Imagine what I might do to her once it's too late for her to retreat."

The pure evil of Jules' grin, the way those piercing eyes burned, Jacques wanted nothing more than to kill the dog and be done with it. Hating that he couldn't... just *yet*. "I will have you sedated and fitted with a feeding tube."

Piercing blue eyes returned to the Commodore. "You can try."

The Beta had not eaten in five days, was no doubt weak from starvation, and very much in need of a serious beating. One Jacques could not administer without causing further distress to his mate now that he understood that her bond to the Beta was just as weighty as her bond to him. A minor annoyance that would be handled soon enough. "Consider it done."

Unfolding in a graceful, sinuous motion, the Beta stalked to the glass between them. "I can tell by the fact that you stand this close to the glass that you truly have no idea of who I am or what I am capable of. The Omega is uncomfortable, because your botched attempts to poison me have failed, yet she eats. She sleeps. You are whining over an inconvenience to a woman who will hate you either way. And you are coming to terms with the fact that this situation did not unfold as you expected. The greatest mistake you have ever made was tempting me with a taste of her. And I will see that you pay for it."

Something about the trapped Beta's threat unsettled Jacques deeply—the honesty that rang through the tiny sliver of the man he could feel. The dead-eyed stare. "I could make your life here one of luxury. It is in Brenya's best interest that I do so. As an act of good faith, I have let you watch me fuck her. What if I were also to have her used clothing sent to your cell so you can smell sweet slick? I will even send you a skilled Beta female to mount. She can simulate the experience. I am only asking that you eat and end this charade. I cannot let you starve to death any more than I can let you walk free as you are."

"To be clear—" Jules smirked, languidly rolling a shoulder as if he were already amidst a flawless carnal experience. "—when I fuck Brenya Perin, I will show her heights your fumbling ineptitude will never approach. And after I have ruined her for all men, it will be my name she screams when you force your way into her nest."

A very Alpha growl filled the air at such slander. It left Jacques swelling in stature, a snarl on his face. "You forget that I bore witness to how little finesse you showed when you rammed your Beta cock up my sweet Omega's ass. I have tasted the pleasures of that hole since, so I understand why you roared and tore at her throat. We fucked her together, but you were something else entirely. Inhuman in your slathering cult language. It took five of my best Alphas to tear you from her after she had passed out. So many tranquilizers I am amazed you still breathe."

And Jacques now understood why the pair of them had awoken in unison the following day. Their Omega-Beta connection ran on a very physical level. And that would be handled. Now that he grasped what he was dealing with, it would be handled immediately.

So he feigned, "Perhaps another day or two of starvation will make you more reasonable. Consider my offer. There could be a life for you here, once you fall in line. A new Beta every day to satiate your urges, as many males or females as you wish. Projections of Brenya to remind you of the gift I bestowed upon you."

An image alighted on the glass between them, sparked into false reality by the translucent life-size three dimensions.

Brenya bloomed into clarity—shy, reserved, delicate.

Smiling at the projection of his mate, knowing the exact moment he had captured her perfection, Jacques reached out as if to touch Brenya, standing in the breeze of his balcony right as the perfect gust of wind softly led the hair about her face to dance. Her dress shaping to her form and highlighting exceptional breasts. It was the same projection that played over and over on his desk when he attended to his duties and could not be with her.

And he was sharing this to tame the rabid dog whose violence almost unseated Jacques' knot as the link was forged.

"Isn't she beautiful?"

The Beta had yet to glance toward the gift. So Jacques sweetened the offering.

Brenya resting, alone, in his bath. Milky water lapped at pert nipples, the Omega fingering her scabbed bite marks on her shoulder and neck, staring off into space.

Just as he suspected, the Beta could not resist a quick glance. Those unnerving blue eyes focused solely on the claiming mark that had almost ripped Brenya's neck in half.

This monumental moment, the reason this projection has been chosen, offered Ambassador Jules Havel an opportunity to view his work outside of the rut. Physical proof that these games would end and he would learn his place. That vicious mark had purchased the Beta a life of unending pleasures… if only he would adapt to new circumstances.

"I will not be unkind to your position, Jules Havel. In fact, I am eager to indulge your cravings."

The image of Brenya soaking in the tub melted away into a new scene. Gloriously naked, Jacques' Omega straddled his lap, taking his girth, her pupils blown despite her ability to fully seat him in her cunt. Yet her body was dragged down, impaling her deeper still as Jacques maneuvered her at his whim. Though her hands tried to brace against his chest, all of her was bounced with his strength and her resistance—small breasts bobbing, hair flying, her mouth open as an unexpected orgasm arrived before he might knot. He drove forward and locked them together, her head lolling back to feel her Alpha bloom in the sweetest cunt. Eyes went wide, the Omega rolling her hips as if she might glean more as her belly expanded from his come as if her tiny body had not tried to unseat and deny an organ so large.

Jacques had been so proud.

Watching it, though he had viewed this moment dozens of times, made his cock pulse to life. Proud and throbbing against his trousers, his erection leaked, waiting to be choked and drained. Always ready for her, and Jacques had nothing but pleasure in knowing the Beta could see but not touch.

"You can feel when she climaxes, so you'll know that

once I return to the nest, I will take her in this exact way and prepare a new projection for you. There is no shame in pleasuring yourself, knowing such a generous gift will arrive. Eat, and I will see that you are furnished with a slick-drenched pillow from her nest and a Beta to fuck on it."

13

It should have occurred to Brenya sooner. In Palo Corps, her duty had been to identify defects and repair them. Rarely was the damage as simple as a poorly fitted connection or faulty wiring. Yet even if it was, when an engineering grunt made *the descent*, their duty was to know that every moment they risked exposure, everyone under the glass depended on them.

The entirety of the infrastructure had to be considered. During the climb, if dust was found on a solar collection, it was the grunt's duty to polish it in passing. If the wind had carried some bracken that stuck to the glass, it would be removed.

Mated to the Commodore of Bernard Dome… her days were now spent under the weight of a large Alpha with a constant erection. She braced. Trying to survive—knowing George had suffered, knowing the lives of Annette and her baby might end at any moment, hiding as often as she was able in the mindscape of such utter darkness, Brenya knew what Jacques had failed to grasp.

It wasn't just George, or Annette, or little Matthieu.

Everyone under the Dome was in danger, and it was Jacques' doing.

And it had to be undone.

She could have told the Alpha these things, but he had proven himself incapable of listening past his own flawed judgment. Her voice to him only mattered if it was to please his ego, to thank him for something she had not asked for and didn't want.

That is what it meant to be the most powerful woman in Bernard Dome. It meant diamonds locked around your neck and silence in the presence of Alphas.

White dresses, sweet wine, boredom, unease, and the constant job of supplicating the male who had admitted he hurt her during sex so she would fight back.

Because she had not touched him when he was inside her? No one had told her she was supposed to touch him. Ancil had strictly ordered her to bend over and brace.

Annette was right, there was nowhere to run. Jacques would always follow.

This was going to be her life, until the life went out of her.

And it already felt like she was being pushed to the wayside by Jacques' mental invasions and Jules' yawning emptiness. An overbearing presence in juxtaposition to a man whose soul had been scooped out.

Gnawing hunger that grew worse by the day. *The dust on the solar collector she had missed.* A total failing in her duty to the Dome.

Ambassador Jules Havel was starving.

And she could feel it as real as if it were her own guts crying out for sustenance.

The same man who had witnessed her public warning to Annette not to eat the Beta rations she had been served at his state dinner. The Thólosen terrorist knew the food wasn't clean.

Jacques couldn't see the endless unfeeling void of the man like she could. He didn't understand that poking his rabid dog was going to kill them all. Jacques didn't know that Jules had a Rebecca.

And if he was even as slightly obsessed with the woman as Jacques was with Brenya, the Dome was going to suffer all the sooner.

"You are tormenting me with your indifference."

The moment Brenya understood how much she had overlooked by wallowing in her own unchanging misery, she set down her golden fork. Abandoning the remaining pasta Jacques had served for dinner, she couldn't bear to look at the man for another moment. "I think I am going to be sick."

The Commodore's complaints about her lack of engagement when he mounted her and her indifference to his existence evaporated, Jacques rising from his chair as if coming closer to her would be anything other than unsettling.

The purr was loud, forceful—rapid in a way that almost

leaned toward panic. Yet his arms were oddly gentle as he helped her stand.

The dinner was deserted to the evening air, the golden fork with so many possibilities forgotten, as it had been forgotten each night. After all, every maintenance panel hidden behind the papered walls of the Commodore's bedroom had been sealed beyond her ability to open them.

Not that Brenya had tried. She could smell the epoxy.

The myriad of buttons that ran down the back of her dress were undone with hurried expertise, freeing Brenya of another hated dress with the finesse of a man who must have done so for other women many times. Usually, he just rent her clothing from neck to navel. Usually, the Alpha was more concerned with licking cream from her nipples as dessert than he was with treating her clothing with respect.

The man liked to break things, he liked the noises she made when he uncovered flesh in the most violent of ways.

He liked to hold her down in the nest and pour sweet things on skin. He liked to lap and suck and leave marks with his teeth.

But at her statement of illness, she had been offered a reprieve.

Instead of fucking her, again, he pressed her back to the mattress and thought to touch in a way that seemed as if he practiced intimacy. The strokes of his large, warm hands were long. His purr was masculine and determined.

Lulled into a quiet place, cautious that he would alter his intention and use her like he did his napkin at dinner, Brenya floated in mental stillness.

He believed her asleep.

Brenya encouraged this by retreating to that emptiness where she could hide uninvited, eyes closed and breath soft. And a miracle was delivered.

Shifting his weight off the bed as if trying not to wake her, Jacques went to his dressing room. Moments later, he had quietly abandoned the room.

Opening her eyes to blissful solitude, Brenya invaded another man's emotionless void further. Leaning on the wrongness of Jules to hide what she intended to do.

She slipped from an unsatisfying arrangement of blankets and pillows, bare feet landing on a soft rug.

If smiles were something natural in Central, Brenya would have smiled to see that Jacques had left his day's clothing on the floor beside the bed. The vanity of the Alpha was so extreme he donned fresh things to confront what made Brenya sick.

Obsessive as he was, there was no other logical alternative for his behavior.

Jacques' abandoned shirt became hers, the only piece of utilitarian clothing that had touched her skin in ages.

Just like the sloppy leavings of his apparel on the ground, the male had forgotten to lock the door to his private balcony. He had not considered that a golden fork was priceless beyond its polished glitter as one twirled their pasta in the bowl of a matching golden spoon.

The unused knife was almost as exciting.

Priceless china and crystal goblets were abandoned for the simplicity of dumping leftovers atop the starched napkin

Jacques had told her was to be laid in the lap and used to dab the mouth should a sauce turn rogue.

Foolish.

Fabric of this nature, with its tight weave and stiffness, was much better knotted up at the corners. Brenya made a tool from a frivolous thing. Just as she took the stolen shirt on her back and wound the tails that hung almost to her feet into a sling.

Careless if Central's fancy cuisine was mushed into one soggy mass, Brenya tucked the pack in her makeshift pouch and snatched up the only tools she would have for what had to be done.

Just as she would have bit down on any tool when her hands needed to be free during maintenance, she pinched the golden necks of her utensils between her teeth.

Hands braced on the wide balustrade, she took a steadying breath, then stepped out onto the ledge.

All of this having been done so quickly, unit 17C would have outshined her class in efficiency and received a red ribbon of excellence. All of it done with her mind on the plane of emotionless function so familiar, so missed, that she dared not enjoy the splendor of freedom from feeling.

Standing, Brenya towered over Central, the updraft sending her hair into disarray. Her city was at her feet, her people going about their lives, oblivious to Central's machinations and their Commodore's flaws.

Exactly how it needed to remain.

Yet Jacques already had a head start.

Fortunately, the palace was intricately embellished with

cavorting depictions of the Gods, complicated architectural details offering footholds aplenty. She didn't even need a rope.

Gold utensils in her teeth and a bag of leftover food stowed in her stolen shirt, she braced her weight on her left foot for leverage... and ascended.

Hands and feet moving from one unlikely grip to another, Brenya moved in a horizontal line, tracking the path Jacques would have had to make to leave his apartments.

At the third window, she glimpsed Jacques moving down a corridor. He would soon be out of her sight. All she needed was a single access panel. Having stood on this balcony, uninterrupted while Jacques stared at her, Brenya knew exactly where to go.

Hand burning with the familiar exercise of holding up her entire body weight, she dangled by a single hand and slipped the knife from her teeth. With the perfect pressure and leverage, the panel popped in.

Slipping into the dimly illuminated maintenance shaft, Brenya stalked the scent of her mate through the air vents as he strolled toward the centralized lift. Guards. Flanking doors as gold as the knife in her hand. She watched them call the elevator as she unscrewed access to the vertical shaft. As if Jacques was above such a menial task.

The lift had already begun to descend before she pulled away the panel. Knife and fork back between her teeth, she sucked a deep breath through her nostrils, wiped her palms on her stolen shirt, and counted to three.

Rocking back on her heels, she jumped.

A moment of blissful freefall. Floating and weightless. Burdened only with gravity and one chance to catch the cables before her.

It was if she had been born for this, the ease in which that rope of engineered steel found her palms. How her skin burned when her body's momentum continued forward only to be jerked back by a sure grip.

She'd done it!

Of course she had. She was Brenya Perin, who had once breathed outside air and climbed the Dome with one working arm.

She was so much more than a kept pet used to satisfy the sexual urges of a bad man.

The most powerful woman in Bernard Dome.

As the elevator continued its rapid descent, her hair flew upward as she cut through the air, alighted to the cable that bore her weight as if she were the butterfly landing on the side of her beloved Bernard Dome.

Sublevel G2.

The lift slowed, stopped, and Brenya closed her eyes.

All buildings under the Dome followed the same standard engineering code, there were no secrets in design. Making it simple to visualize where she was in regards to Jacques' rooms.

A map bloomed in her thoughts.

And then she moved.

A short climb down the cable led to a soft landing on the top of the elevator car. From there, she took to the steel maintenance ladder and made her way to the nearest access panel.

Spidering through the ducts, unsure of which direction Jacques may have taken, she thought she might have lost him.

Until she heard a male voice, almost imperceptible right below where she crept. Ear to the metal, she made out Jacques' threat.

"I will have you sedated and fitted with a feeding tube."

"You can try."

The voice of Ambassador Jules Havel.

Pulling her ear from the ground, Brenya set her tools before her and strategized.

Unless there was a different maintenance corridor that serviced the room. The ducting in that area had not been designed to be easily deconstructed. Such efficiency in design was only used for rooms that required little ventilation. She didn't even see plumbing in the tight space.

Even the electrical wiring was scarce.

Ambassador Jules Havel had been tucked into a storage bay.

Ignoring the muffled incompressible sound of male voices below, knife and fork were used to dissect the panel beneath her—dismantling the shaft's floor as delicately as she would a damaged pane outside the Dome.

14

Breath held, Brenya pried the loose plate free, sliding the square as silently as she might to the side. It was dim in what was clearly a converted storage space. An unreliable source of light offered a low, unsteady glow—changing color and output while doing little to break through the shadows.

Illuminated by that scant flicker, Brenya found…

A single cell.

A single prisoner.

No guard posted within the room.

Brown tangles trailing toward the ground, she ignored the staring Beta absorbing everything an upside-down room might provide.

The stink of Jacques' anger lingered in his absence, as did the scent of her slick—slick he'd rubbed into his skin one of the several times he had mounted her earlier that day.

It was not a pleasant smell.

Yet, it was nothing to the horror of unacceptable design on display.

The haphazardly constructed containment would have led to reassignment, had any engineering grunt from Palo Corps installed the travesty. The entire construct of Jules' prison was one massive flaw in workmanship. A sheet of the amorphous metal that made up the *glass* of the Dome had been assaulted by a drill, pinned to concrete with screws. Screws! No human eye might see them, but undoubtedly each drilled hole was surrounded by a mass spider web of microscopic cracks.

These were incredibly strong yet brittle fabrications.

They required the perfect nest into their surroundings. They were built to melt into one another.

That is why, from outside, the Dome looked as if it were one solid half circle of glass. A gently curved, elegant construction of painstakingly crafted pieces… as if the Dome itself were one organism.

To have drilled screws through a single panel to hold those plates in place? An immediate failure in the integrity of the entire structure. To expect screws to hold the weight of that microscopically cracking panel was sheer stupidity of the most insulting sort.

What a waste and ruin of an excellent resource.

Had the Beta behind the glass taken the time to test his cage, he would have learned that enough force near either wall would damage his containment to a point it would have eventually shattered.

The clarity of that glass, a sure sign that Ambassador Jules Havel had not attempted to fight his way out.

He'd *allowed* what was being done to him.

Why?

Brenya had seen that specific shade of blue before, the flashing indigo of Jules Havel's eyes—at the center of a lightning strike. It had been one of the most catastrophic storms to smash against the Dome. Two long days by reinforcing a great deal of damage from the inside of the glass, ignoring the amber glow of fire where the woods smoldered in the rain.

It was the blue of impending destruction, Jules saying nothing so loudly, it was as if he acknowledged her assessment.

She had not been prepared to find a willing prisoner who starved voluntarily, but it seemed this male—this Thólosen terrorist—was plotting. All the more reason to finish this now.

Setting golden tools back between her teeth, Brenya poured out of the hole she had created in the ceiling. Unfolding until her body was in alignment for an easy landing.

Fingers setting her free of the cramped space, she fell, landing softly in a crouch.

Glancing up, it finally sank in what her view from above had distorted, the source of flickering light.

There was something in the room far uglier than a man incarcerated or the ramshackle prison itself.

She was there. Every last ugly inch of her was on display

in morbid obscenity—her body writhing while it was forcibly dragged down a cock that didn't fit. Until it did.

The size of her made to seem so tiny in comparison to the man who bounced her on his cock. The woman in the projection threw back her head, bowed her back as if inviting the villain deeper. She had parted her lips, sucking down air in a silent, telling gasp.

The gold utensils fell from Brenya's teeth, clanging against standard concrete as they bounced about her naked toes.

"Don't look at it, Brenya."

How could she possibly look away?

Hands with the power to climb across the side of a palace, to have found and held the cable of a moving lift, crept around her middle. As if she might hold in the shame.

The woman in the ongoing display of sexual aggression *enjoyed* herself. Rocking her hips in time with the onslaught, bracing and angling so labia stretched and seeped slick down a pulsating male part, displaying her engorged clitoris for the man to address.

How could she have done what played in that projection? Hair wild, chest heaving, hips circling as if starved for more... she invited the very thing she loathed. How could she have behaved in such a way, when Jacques did what he did?

Twin tears warmed Brenya's cheeks, her breath caught on an uneven inhale.

"Look at me. Look at me, Brenya."

What difference would that make?

"He can make you think its pleasure—an unfair biological advantage."

That silently moaning, unrestrained creature … was a betrayal to Brenya's very being. Action in the exact opposite of feeling. That hideous thing came on a burgeoning knot, shaking as if she had touched a livewire. To see the muscles in her abdomen ripple, to know what was taking place inside her even as the projection's belly began to gently expand.

There was wetness even then between her bare legs. There was always something dripping out of her, because Jacques shot deep and he shot often enough that her very womb had adapted to drink down the deluge.

Old and new seed was in her, growing more liquid by the hour and escaping in a telling, awful trail in that very moment right down her thigh. Pressing her legs together as if that might actually hold it in, Brenya turned wet honey eyes to the man waiting for the rebuke she deserved.

Jules spoke. "Your neck is bleeding."

It was not a question, so it required no answer. It required no attention.

Licking dry lips, unsure where to begin, Brenya cocked her head, aware her expression was one of despondent confusion.

So he spoke for her. "This is where you beg me to spare the people of Bernard Dome."

Exactly. She had made her way to Ambassador Jules Havel for that reason alone.

The cork holding back her voice popped, Brenya stepping closer to the glass. "If I could find humor in this situation, it would be in knowing that we share a secret that shouldn't be a secret at all."

He didn't move. He didn't emote. But he conveyed an ocean of danger. "And what would that be?"

Fingers working the knots she had created in the stolen shirt, the parcel of food she had brought for him was set free. It was in doing that task, in focusing on something other than the strange way the man looked at her, that Brenya was able to tell the truth. "From the moment my life was infected by Jacques Bernard, he has inflicted pain upon me *every single day*. Resisting led to no alteration in this pattern. Surrender led to no change. The pair-bond…"

What was there to even say about the pair-bond? Nothing, because ultimately, it didn't matter. What mattered was Jacques' oversight.

She laughed in the way of the weary and the broken. "The Alpha believes the pair-bond will force you to do everything in your power to keep me safe. And therefore, all of Bernard Dome will be protected from… you."

Her laughter died. Not because the stoic, staring Beta stood unmoving as he absorbed all she did. It was because none of this was funny.

"Like Jacques, you are under no restraint from causing me harm. Pair-bond or no, you would do so in full understanding of your actions. The Commodore has not contained you with his ploy. He has unleashed you on a population who should not be held accountable for my crimes and Jacques' cruelty."

The corner of his mouth twitched up, a contrived expression that conveyed nothing, because the man felt nothing. "You are right. I would hurt you without restraint."

Melting into the glass between them, letting it bear her weight, Brenya shut her eyes to all of it. "I find it reassuring."

"Look at me, Brenya."

Lashes lifting, she obeyed.

Finding that he moved with the precision of a panther, easy grace and coiled violence. That in those few peaceful moments he had fully approached, that he too pressed against it, as if there were nothing between them. As if his hands were already around her throat. And then he whispered as if his breath might warm her ear. "Let me out, and I will hurt you all you like."

A strange shiver left the tiny hairs on the back of her neck to rise. Pushing far enough away from the glass so she might run her attention over everything from the fall of his brown hair, the shape of his ear, the height of his cheekbones, the cruelty of his mouth, to a neck that was tattooed with such dark markings it was as if the evil inside him was trying to claw its way out. "Did you destroy Thólos Dome?"

He answered, "Yes."

"Did you invade Greth?"

Again. "Yes."

Pressing her palm to the faulty installment between them, Brenya stroked the glass. "When I stole your ship, it never occurred to me that you might be on it. I was unaware of the situation in Thólos or the consequence of my choice to seek asylum there. Ultimately, it doesn't matter that I was ignorant and careless. I am fully culpable for this situation."

Fingertips seeking out the secrets of the glass, Brenya digested the nature of what stood physically between them. All the while, lifting her eyes to a terrible, blue, intolerant gaze. "I am sorry, Jules Havel."

"So you have brought me a bag of food to make amends?"

There wasn't time for tricks or word play. There wasn't time for much. They both knew he had not so much as glanced at the food since she arrived.

Swallowing, she dared ask, "Why did you torment the people of Thólos?"

Setting his fingers to the glass, following her exploration of its secrets—as if they shared a strange dance—his voice held an enticing edge. "You know precisely why I slaughtered a civilization."

"Bernard Dome is not like Thólos." Nor was she empty and soulless like the man before her. "My people are blameless, peaceful, hardworking, dedicated—everything opposite of those you have been exposed to in Central."

"Conveniently anesthetized into the perfect slave labor."

The Beta was not exactly right, and he was not exactly wrong. But there was no point in debating what the man had never experienced.

"If I return you to your Rebecca, will you forgive me for what was done to you and leave my people alone?"

"No."

"I understand." And she did. She understood in a strangely malignant way.

Their dance was over, Brenya having found the slot that

might be coaxed open so that a Beta prisoner could be given food and water. The programming sequence to open it had not been modified from the same she had used all her years making conducting repairs during the descent. Another sign Jacques had no concept of how his Dome actually functioned.

Brenya would not even need to break the glass to get Jules out.

Fingers moving in a dedicated pattern, it began to slide open, wider and wider, like a waterfall parting when a hand cut through its stream.

"This is just remarkably lazy." All muttered under her breath as she bent down to scoop up the parcel of food.

He had her before she might blink, Brenya's wrist caught, her body dragged forward until once again she was pressed up to the barrier between them.

Food hit the ground in its soaked napkin with a splat… on the wrong side of the glass. It was the other hand he had stolen, the other arm he used to maneuver her where he wished.

Parts of her that were sore and swollen were soothed by the chill of the glass. Parts of her that were fire and frightened resisted. There was no undoing it.

Gripping her wrist tight enough to negate her struggles, the edge of Jules' fingernail dragged a light path from the hollow of her elbow down the inside of her arm.

Unable to recover her arm from that calloused touch, she growled, "We don't have time for this!"

"Speak for yourself. I have eternity." Jules stopped

tracing the veins in her arm to toy with her fluttering fingers instead. "That is what a pair-bond is. Forever, Brenya Perin."

Angry with the man, Brenya snarled, "Jules Havel of Thólos, I am begging you. I cannot save you all if you do not stop this and come with me now. The more time we waste, the less of a chance I can even get you outside. Not to mention that I will have to build a transmitter from stolen parts as we move so your people will be aware of your location in the woods. Let go of my arm!"

"Beg." Reaching through the glass, he took a handful of her stolen shirt, pulling her closer still. "That is what you came here to do, isn't it?"

This was unacceptable, infuriating. "You will never get out of the Dome without my help."

With her cheek to the glass and his body pressed to the other side as if he might seep through it and take her any way he wished, Jules laughed. A true laugh she could not see. An expression on his face that was denied her. Which, for some reason, stung. "This virtuous help which comes at the price of saving... who?"

Fine, she could admit she wanted more from the Beta than only grace toward her people and to send him home. She needed him. "Unspeakable things have been done to my friends."

"Annette?"

He loosened his grip enough that she might maneuver back and glare. "Yes."

"Who else?"

"Her child. He will be murdered soon to make way for

Ancil's new baby. The child might even already be dead. But I will not stand by and wait for it to happen like everyone else in this hell." Yanking her hand free and rubbing her wrist as if she might chase off the odd tingles he'd encouraged there, Brenya hissed, "You need me if you want to return to your Rebecca. I need you to help my friends. Shelter a woman and her child in the woods until Greth ships arrive. I know the air outside is clean. And, so long as I remain behind, Jacques will not think to search outside the Dome. He'll be too distracted punishing me to realize until it's too late."

"No."

Frustration led her to bang a curled fist against the glass. Scooping up the food that had fallen from her hand when he yanked her off-center, she threw the pack in his cell. In a practiced gesture that screamed disappointment, Brenya sealed the pane, watching the man ignore her offering, choosing instead to take a seat on the floor and lean against the side wall.

He stared forward as if she had never been there. As if projections of her did not cycle beside where they had argued.

When she failed to retreat, her lip trembling in exasperation, he said, "If I were you, I would run back to my nest and hide."

15

GRETH DOME

"Segment AA-14." Gray eyes traced the movement of the agitated Commodore, an Alpha who lacked the most basic semblance of control. Blond hair as long as a woman's ran loose behind him, and he stomped through his halls, the embroidery of his jacket something from a long-dead culture. The way the man continued to fiddle with his cuffs, a tell—his confrontation with Jules Havel had given the man no satisfaction. "Draw him there. Disrupt all safety protocols to the east of Ms. Perin."

"But that's not the direction she came." Fingers flying over the controls, Maryanne dripped with nervous sweat in an effort to keep up with the Shepherd's commands. "The Omega took the opposite corridor, and I can only turn off one at a time without drawing attention to the *massive amount of infiltration I am conducting* in Bernard's Palace. Even if I am only operating against a computer, these logs will be noticed!"

"The Omega now knows where she is in relation to the structure. She won't take the same path to return to Jacques' den. Watch." And he was correct. She crawled to the east corridor to access a vertical chute, climbing in a blur that would leave her hands blistered. "And you will remove all traces of our interference once we have assured she reaches her destination undetected."

"What she doesn't know is that the only reason she hasn't been caught is because I am fucking slaving away." There wasn't even time for Maryanne to brush loose hair off her brow. "For future reference, Shepherd, this kind of work takes at least three people. One person cannot manage five levels of security protocols with no advance notice and with no idea what they are dealing with alone!"

Unmoved by the woman's theatrics, Shepherd ordered, "Eyes on the Commodore. Start an electrical fire to his left."

Entering a series of commands, sparks ignited—bulbs bursting as the voltage was manually increased beyond safe levels. Easy enough, though suspicious if anyone in that Dome had a brain cell between them.

As if stunned so simple a trick worked, Maryanne muttered, "Who still uses fucking lightbulbs anymore?"

"Men who wish to display their ability to waste a resource for the sake of vanity and as a show of power."

Cocking a brow, Maryanne reached for a COM, cycling to a new display. "Are there lightbulbs in your new palace?"

Shepherd didn't so much as blink at the question, his focus on the multitude of active screens. "Yes."

"Let me guess. Claire thinks they are pretty."

"For someone who demanded two assistants because she lacks the ability to handle this duty alone, I would suggest you prove to me that you are not so easily replaceable."

"Who else on your team could have watched over that girl before you even got to the room? She climbed half naked across the side of a building! Guards were everywhere on the ground and I was manning this station while you were fast asleep." Pursing her lips on an exhale when the latest integration of the system almost failed, Maryanne added, "You didn't even get here until she jumped for the elevator—which was admittedly badass. So toss me some credit, I'm not even sure how I was able to dial your COM with that spider monkey on the loose."

"Stop talking and pay attention. The Commodore has extinguished the fire, and guards are swarming around him. Standard procedure will lead to a lockdown of the grounds." Despite the inability of the woman to remain quiet, Shepherd's focus was unbroken. His enemy under his thumb. It didn't matter that there was an ocean between them, that they existed in two separate Domes. They may as well have stood eye-to-eye.

Any man who had dared met Shepherd's gaze in hostility had already lost. A few hours more and the Commodore would feel the fingers already around his throat squeezing until he was made to kneel.

"Intact Dome containment protocol in staging area base

one. Assist the containment protocols if for any reason they fail or manual override is enacted, no one gets out. Record everything in that building."

"That isn't in the Palace, Shepherd. I don't even have that sector of the Dome on screen right now." Flying to another set of controls, Maryanne scrambled to follow. "Well damn, it might as well be a palace. Look at all that loot."

Shutters fell about a startled group of men smoking cigars while the pretty Beta serving their cocktails dropped her tray.

"Enter code: *Saga Culprit Kiss*." There was no hesitation or remorse in Shepherd's cold command. There was only a job to be done. "Release the virus."

Maryanne's fingers stopped flying over the assortment of controls at her disposal, and for the first time in an hour, her attention left the screens. Though his attention never wavered from the multitude of live screens before him, he registered the nervous shake of her head in negation of his order.

She even whispered, "I can't... I can't do that."

Pushing her aside with easy effort, Maryanne's chair rolled from the console, and Shepherd took charge. And with a single keystroke, five people in a single building were infected with Red Consumption.

What had been confusion and lighthearted laughter at a technical glitch became Alphas scrambling from their chairs at the sound of a canister hiss. As with untried men, infighting was immediate. Shepherd did not need to hear the accusation thrown between them, he had witnessed the behavior hundreds of times over the years of his campaign.

They were blaming one another, some leaning on the idea that it was a prank, a power play to intimidate the very rivals who smoked together, sipping dark liquor.

The oldest of them began to cough.

They could not possibly imagine what poison they breathed or how quickly it would kill them, but some deep animal part of them understood. They began to frantically beat at the shutters and attempt to use their COM, breaking furniture in an attempt to create a tool that could defeat steel.

From contented banter to abject terror… in less than three minutes.

Containment held.

The group would be dead in less than an hour. Lying in their glittering clothes, in their glittering club, in pools of glittering red contaminated blood. Their loved ones would never be able to collect the bodies. Their enemies would have no corpse to spit at.

Every treasure in that room would be burned to ash.

As if she had yet to come to terms with who she served, Maryanne muttered in horror, "You just murdered five people."

Shepherd's focus never wavered, he continued to do the job. "I murder at least five people every day."

For a moment, the air stank of sour fear, Maryanne audibly swallowing. Hesitant in returning to her duty—a woman who had undoubtedly killed when it had served her in Thólos—she went back to the controls.

"You have grown soft in seclusion, Maryanne Cauley." Because she had been coddled and comforted. "Never forget that I know precisely why you were thrown into the Undercroft."

"This is different." Her voice betrayed her trepidation far more than her stink ever would. "That was *personal*. This is… anyone could have been in that club tonight. You have no idea who you killed."

"That task will fall to you once Brenya Perin has reached her final destination undetected. Get back on task and spare me your false scruples."

"Staring at corpses who've puked out their lungs sounds like a great way to be rewarded. Even Jules was offered a Beta to fuck." Dexterous fingers began flying over the controls, the female's snark returning with a "Where the fuck is my Beta? And, for your information, *mon capitaine*, you turned off the containment protocol notification. No one is going to know those people were infected. Your distraction is pointless."

"At no time did I claim it was a distraction."

"So, you just killed them because?"

How she still failed to wrap her head around it, Shepherd would have to address another time. "Brenya Perin has reached her exit point. She did this after scuttling her way through foreign surroundings to find Jules and offer him easy freedom. She did this with only a fork and a knife. I have fitted you with the best technology in Greth Dome, and you have lost Jacques Bernard, because your focus is pathetic."

"Fuck!" Scrambling to switch the feed, Maryanne leaned on facial recognition software—a desperate fallback that would take more time than they had. The voice of his student wavered as if she fought to hold it together after the intensity of the last hour. "Wait. Brenya is in the wrong location. She's climbed higher than her rooms."

Again, the Alpha female had missed the point, Shepherd explaining as if Maryanne were a simpleton. "She's tired and she thinks she might fall. The balcony will catch her."

Together, they watched an Omega with a fork and knife pry open an access panel and suck in outside air. Unlike Maryanne, she didn't waste time. Brenya ripped open her shirt, stripped fully naked, and stuffed the dirty thing behind her. Climbing out, one foot on the winged shoulder of the Omega Goddess, the other notched into a bit of filigree, she closed the panel and hastened to screw it shut.

Panting from the effort, favoring her right arm, she slid down the wall. There was no way for her to see at that speed where she might land her weight, what handholds might become available, but instinct drove her to find a path before she fell a greater distance than she might survive unscathed.

Shepherd and Maryanne watched as the final foothold was missed.

Dangling from one arm, the Omega took the utensils out of her teeth and let go.

The landing was hard; there would be further bruising. But her Alpha didn't seem the type who would notice the changing landscape of her skin.

Fork and knife were back on the empty table just as Jacques entered the room. Finding his mate missing from the nest, he raced toward the open door to the balcony.

Shepherd issued another order. "Give me volume."

"What are you doing out here?" The Commodore looked at the breathless woman, turning his glare next to the forgotten dinner table. *"Did you eat all that food while I was gone?"*

She didn't answer, sitting down in the nearest chair with her hands folded in her lap.

"I asked you a question, mon chou."

Brenya Perin stared down at her fingers, struggling to keep her breath even. *"I'm very hungry."*

A lie. For on the screen pulled up beside the five angles of Jacques Bernard's rooms, Jules had just finished devouring the food he'd been given.

Not that the people of Bernard Dome would ever know. As per protocol while incarcerated, the Beta had sat still for so many days that playing his actions on a loop would go unnoticed. Had gone unnoticed by the remote guards monitoring his cell.

Tearing at blond hair, the Commodore turned into his room to snarl into a COM where his Omega might not hear. *"Feed him clean food. Whatever he wants. NOW!"*

Then the Alpha was again outside, snatching up the female to return her to the nest. Her back hit the pillows, her hair splayed, and her body laid out like a sacrifice. Standing over her, the male took his time undressing, staring down at the woman as if unsure where to begin the feast. From the feral look of him, it would not be the gentle touch she clearly needed at the moment.

It wasn't until the Alpha crept over her body that Shepherd commanded, "As soon as Jacques Bernard falls asleep, summon him for an emergency meeting with the Chancellor of Greth Dome. Should he refuse, release the footage of the infected gentlemen's club."

At that, Shepherd turned away from the screens. There was no need to watch another man rape Jules' mate... again.

∽

THE DOOR to their bedchamber possessed no lock, but that didn't mean his little one might not have shifted furnishings to keep him from the room. They had not spoken since their argument in the garden, each choosing to coexist in strained silence as he plotted his next move and she belligerently dug in her heels.

It was an easy thing to do when a pair-bond was as strong as theirs, but it was also unacceptable.

Shepherd loved his Claire in a way he'd never fully understand. She was the best kind of addiction, the constant vibration of her being always with him, taking up the space in his chest where most men might have a soul.

She had improved him from the moment he had seen her in those filthy, reeking clothes. There would be no existing without her. If that meant he could only have her in this pretty cage she'd contained herself within, then he would take whatever scraps she might offer.

Not that he would ever cease working to give her everything she ever desired.

Swinging the door easily open, Shepherd found her awake in her nest. Knees under her chin as she stared off into the sunrise. Green eyes that had the power to undo him with a glance rested on her view of their garden. Following her gaze, he realized he had not had the time to tend to her plants before she might wake.

Maybe she was disappointed. Perhaps she thought him petty enough to abandon the project out of anger.

"You didn't come to bed last night."

It would have been a fine evening indeed to have lain next to her, even if she had denied his attentions. "I was called away."

And he was suddenly very weary. With an uncharacteristic sigh, he walked forward and took a seat on the edge of their mattress. Elbows to his knees, he leaned the weight of his upper body forward and stared out at the sunrise.

A little hand came to rest on his spine. "Shepherd, I'm sorry."

"As am I."

Stroking where his back knotted with tension, she teased, "No, you're not. But I appreciate the sentiment."

Cutting a glance over his shoulder, the man found his wife's smirk and loved her all the more for it. "I am sorry, perfect Claire. I am sorry that none of this worked out as it should have. I am sorry that I have given you sound reason to assume the worst of me in all situations. You are not wrong. I would do the things you say should circumstance require."

Black hair fell around her as she scooted closer, her second hand coming to tend to his back with her first. "Honey, I'm listening. Tell me what's going on."

How she could be so sweet, he'd never know. And this

moment, a moment that came out of love despite the recent stings, would be ruined. Because he was going to ask her something that both of them would hate. "Claire, I need you to tell me everything you can think of regarding an Omega who is mated to an Alpha she hates."

Though it was the middle of the night in Bernard Dome, the sun rose outside Greth, but there was nothing but darkness that came from the mouth of the woman Shepherd loved.

"The pair-bond feels like broken glass you are forced to swallow. It cuts deeper every time you breathe. It kills." The tired-eyed Omega in their nest didn't hesitate to continue. "It killed my mother, though it took over a decade to eat her from the inside out. It has led my friends to kill."

Nona French—murderess and mentor—rotting back in Thólos where she belonged.

Under her hands, a slave to Claire's whims in a way she would never fully accept, Shepherd said, "Go on."

"You cannot imagine what it is like to be utterly powerless at another being's whim."

Oh yes, he could.

Claire hesitated, as if his mate thought to spare him from the very thing he had asked for. "With a single sound, an Alpha can hurt you in ways that cut so deep they never stop bleeding."

There was nothing said Shepherd had not earned. But there was a shade of remorse that he seldom allowed himself to acknowledge.

His little one took pity, resting her cheek to his shoulder

while she kneaded his spine. "I can't give you more if I don't know the context, Shepherd. You and I… we fit. Had the circumstances been different when we met, it would have been an effortless union. You have to tell me what happened if you want me to tell you what to do."

Gathering her up, he lay back in a bland nest, knowing the state of their bed was the biggest statement she might make concerning the arguments of the day. Her weight on him was perfect, the way she instinctively hummed in tune with his soft purr, a balm.

Before he might share a history that didn't belong to him, he gathered up her hair and let its silk slip through his fingers. "Jules was once married to an Omega—"

Claire whispered, stroking his flank, "You were there, spying, when Jules told me about Rebecca. I did not forget the terrible story concerning his sons—how Senator Cantor murdered them in front of her before he forced a pair-bond. How he found his wife, once he was free of the Undercroft, that she begged him to kill her. Jules shot her in the head."

"He did." And his compatriot had returned to the Undercroft a very different man.

Placing her chin to his chest so she might look him in the eyes, his little one asked, "You were surprised Jules told me."

"He would have only done so for good reason, a testament to the effort he has put forward for my sake."

Cautiously playful, Claire teased, "He is your friend, Shepherd. It's okay to acknowledge that you have one besides me."

A strange sensation twisted under Shepherd's ribs. "You would consider me your friend, Claire O'Donnell?"

Sleepy smile, eyes glittering, she said, "My best friend."

Before he knew it, she had coaxed a smile out of him, a rare thing that felt both unpracticed and welcome when they were together. If only he could spend the morning playing with her hair and making soft love to her. Instead—for Jules—he told his wife, his *friend*, tales from the Undercroft.

The disturbing story of two Alphas who had been condemned to the dark. How both of them claimed they had been used by a powerful Beta, tricked into a three-pronged pair-bond. How he had confirmed the information himself once the registries were available to him. How the Omegas had died.

And then he told the story of Brenya Perin, looking at his wife, knowing he would be condemned by the parallels of what he had done to Claire.

He had taken his Claire against her will. He had forced her to know pleasure on his cock. He had harmed her friends. He had shamed her by lying with another. He had failed to keep her and their son safe.

He could not honestly say that what had motivated him in those early months was any different than what motivated Jacques Bernard—Shepherd understood an Alpha's insatiable obsession with a new mate.

Shepherd had made mistakes, but he also had an accounting of every last mark on his Omega's body. There could not have been so much as a splinter he did not know the source of.

There was no meal on her plate that he had not approved. Every article of clothing, every last green dress, was chosen by him. He still dictated her days to an extent that, should Claire ever realize, would upset her.

It would *greatly* upset her. And he had no intention of changing his ways. Ever.

She would always be his number one priority.

And that was the difference between himself and Jacques Bernard. He had put his Omega in danger from the moment he'd forced a pair-bond. And it would never be undone.

Listening with a concentration of someone who understood the weight of his words, she asked relevant questions regarding the stories of the long-dead Alphas, their Omegas, and the Betas who had orchestrated it all.

Gnawing her lip, Shepherd could see what she was thinking, surprised she put a voice to her thoughts.

"In both situations, the Omegas died and the Betas lived." Dropping her voice to a whisper as if the Goddess might not hear her say such a thing, Claire said, "Jules could leave her behind and come home."

Cupping his mate's cheek, Shepherd met her eyes. "If you only knew the things that man had done to return to Rebecca, you would be frightened to stand in his presence. Brenya Perin broke into his cell tonight and offered him a sound chance for escape. Knowing that we could have assured from our end that it took place, Jules refused to go."

"So he wants this woman despite the fact that he cannot ever have her?"

Drawing her cheek down to his chest, increasing the purr,

Shepherd replied, "I saw the way he looked at her, little one. It's the same way I look at you."

"Then it's done, Shepherd."

No. It had only just begun.

A foreign power could not contain Jules Havel. The Commodore of Bernard Dome could not degrade a man who had stood by Shepherd's side, who had been his *friend*—who had charmed Claire when she was lonely, who had stood as his partner as they had wreaked vengeance upon Thólos.

Jacques Bernard had started a war.

And five of his people had already died.

16

BERNARD DOME

He had never seen her eyes so wide upon his return, or found her so eager to run her palms over his body when he reached for his *mon chou*.

She had heard him, grasped that males enjoyed touch, and was listening.

Even if she was sick from too much food.

That first thrust broke the magic, his mate grimacing at the impact of his hips on hers.

Why could she not be like the Beta females he could ride day and night? Fragile vaginal passage, picky womb, there always seemed to be something that hindered what should be between them.

Pulling out, he issued the growl he knew would leave her body pumping out the very fluid it needed to seat him, before he shoved back in.

Deep.

Omegas were designed by the Gods to be fucked and adored by Alphas, but this one, she needed endless work.

Which only made him crave her more.

No pussy would ever panic around his cock like Brenya's did. And when he conquered—as he always did—no pussy would ever choke his knot so hard he saw stars.

She was a strong thing, small breasts thrust toward his mouth as her back bowed.

Her pain made him leak for her. The pleasure he could make her feel would swell her flat stomach until she was fat with him.

Thrusting hard and fast, feeding off her submission and sorry squeaks, he grunted like a boar and fucked.

In his bed.

In his Dome.

His mate.

The Omega thought to supplicate with his latest demands that she touch him. Pats here. Pats there. A great deal of squealing.

He prayed the bastard Beta locked downstairs could feel each thrust. Knowing he might, Jacques ravaged all the harder.

Her ankles at his back, the Omega cried out. "I am begging you!"

Then he would deliver. Lifting his weight from her tiny frame, Jacques sat back on his heels so he might see how perfectly her labia screamed around her mate's cock.

Stretched bloodless, they hugged his shaft as he retreated from her heat. Puffed with the force of his next thrust, that part of her seemed to disappear.

If he didn't know her better, he would assume she was having a stroke.

So he *stroked* her again.

Warm honey, that was what her eyes looked like before he blew them into black.

Hand to slender hips, watching the bouncing tits of his pretty Omega, he fucked and fucked and fucked away—tossing his head back when she began to flutter.

When her pussy began to beg.

As it should!

The knot, perhaps his sixth of the day, was not his most impressive. Still, it locked behind her pubic bone, shot deep and true.

It was genuine, just like the text claimed. Mated Alpha's testicles were always swollen. They needed to be milked.

Jacques had learned this the hard way, moaning as he circled his hips and dug even deeper.

Gods, she was small. When she grew fat with his babies, she would scarce be able to stand upright.

She could hardly contain him as it was!

Which only urged him to fill her even more.

Bones creaking under his hips, she opened enough that his knot might dig deeper.

And deeper still as his perfect female swooned.

That fucking Beta! The arrogance of the man. To think

that he might ever be capable of tasting her sweet slick without Jacques to draw it forth. A mere Beta couldn't make her bloom with a single rumbling note, the application of the perfect force.

Brenya needed an Alpha...

The sleeve encasing his cock began to rhythmically convulse. Little hands touching on his body as if he were a console.

Could a console fuck this hard?

The wayward Omega squealed like a cute little piglet each time he shoved his knot deeper.

That first wad of seed...

It was as if Jacques could feel how thick and globular it might be, traveling down his shaft, his sperm searching for her cervix.

Omegas were meant to drink. All the text said so.

So this one had been conditioned to bloat. Brenya didn't even cry anymore when her tummy got fat. Like any good mate, she lay and accepted.

When his knot inevitably shrank, she even held a good portion deep inside.

He'd tested her more than once. Gently pushing on her tummy to watch the flood he left inside her wet the bed.

It came out curdled these days, solid proof that her sweet cunt wanted to retain what he had graced her with. But there was something about watching his gift flow.

Drinking it down was even better.

Honey.

The perfect slippery sweetness. Sucking her empty, enjoying how she groaned when he brought her to an empty climax, Jacques thought of the Beta trapped below and slurped down a mouthful of himself.

17

BERNARD DOME

Muscles stiff from built-up lactic acid, scraped raw inside and out, bruised—sleep had dragged Brenya down so deep she didn't so much as toss in the sticky puddle of fluids left behind when Jacques finished with her.

The first sharp jerk didn't so much as register. It was the following insistent tugs on her arm that, *oh so slowly*, gave her a reason to part her lashes.

It was still dark, yet a single lamp had been lit, outlining the form of a radiant woman dressed in maroon silks. Pin-straight black locks perfect, almost as smooth as the glass of the Dome.

"You must rise, Commodorina!"

Accent thick, fingernails sharp, a slender figure literally pulled her almost to the floor.

"What?" What on earth could anyone want when there

had been dreams of sandy beaches, jungles outside the Dome? There had been fresh, unrecycled air....

"I was ordered to fetch you. Wash, dress, quickly. Chancellor Shepherd waits for no one." Narrowing her eyes, Lucia clicked her tongue. "You have to answer for what you did."

Her stomach dropped, the sense of failure in duty hardwired into every part of her being. She did need to answer, but not to the men. She needed to answer to Annette.

Defeated, Brenya couldn't even find the energy to snarl at the unexpected and undesired presence. Blinking up at the woman with the perfect sheet of black hair, her aristocratic features and straight nose, her sun-bronzed skin, Brenya found it hard to see her past prejudice. "Lucia."

The Omega was pregnant with Ancil's preferred child. His mate.

"Hate me later, Commmodorina. Bathe now, and dress for royalty. The men wait to judge you, and I will be held accountable if they are not impressed." Lacking all mercy, Lucia yanked her arm again. "Come, come, the bath is already full, and you *stink*."

Even bleary and aching head to toe, from Brenya's position, she had all the leverage, applying the proper force to take back control of her arm.

The very thing she had been unable to do when Jules Havel was the one with his paws on her. It was either set Brenya free, or Lucia was going to end up on the disgusting bed beside her.

The Omega set her free, bracing before she too might end up on that horrendous bed.

Once her footing had been gained, Lucia snarled, raising her head only to bite back whatever she had planned to say.

In their little struggle, the sheet had fallen away, an unobstructed view of Brenya's nude upper body exposed.

Openly staring, Lucia took in all that was on display: the shape of Brenya's breasts, the bruises, the bites, each scrape. Eyes rolling upward, she sighed. "You're one of *those* Omegas. Gods, send me strength." As if to dig some barb that Brenya didn't quite grasp deeper, the woman added, "And your nesting skills are atrocious. You are practically a queen, yet you sleep like a peasant. No wonder Ancil sent me to prepare you. You shame us all!"

Just the sound of Ancil's name set Brenya's teeth on edge. "I have no interest in being prepared. I can be judged as I am."

There was no shame in what she had done, only regret that she had failed Annette and her son. That she had been caught and might never have another opportunity to do what was right.

There was regret in having heard a man cry out for his woman when he was tempted by something as inconvenient as her traitorous pheromones. There was regret in how Brenya had gone to Jules Havel first to make it right. Regret in her failure to understand normal feelings—in assuming the Ambassador cared for Rebecca.

Why else would he have whispered her name?

It had not been Brenya's imagination—the moment, like every moment she had ever lived—was catalogued and memorized. Even now, she could replay the look on his face and the pain in his voice.

Yet he had chosen to stay locked in a cell?

And she now chose to lay in the soggy bed of her own making.

Ignoring the Alpha who yanked at her mind with such force she was little more than a puppet. Rejecting the treacherous Beta's void and the lies within it.

Let them have their icy cold indifference and burning hot anger.

Brenya was done with them both.

Rubbing her sore shoulder, she closed her eyes and allowed herself a deep breath. Then another, too tired to care.

Fingers repeatedly snapped in her face, Lucia saying, "We are all aware that you are unpolished, but I didn't assume you were also dimwitted. Men of this level do not wait on one foolish Omega."

No, they didn't. "I'm ready."

Lucia's beauty was not marred by her irritated expression. "*You are naked.*"

Did it matter anymore? She had just crept through the palace bare from the waist down. Projections of her writhing in a sexual encounter were playing on repeat for a prisoner in a shoddy cell. Modesty had yet to apply in her new existence.

"I'm always naked."

A trill of aggressive foreign language followed, Lucia moving to the dressing room to pick through the uncomfortable clothing that hung from every last rail—so many dresses. Brenya had not even worn a portion of them. She had not so much as entered that room. Jacques picked all of it.

Out of sight, Lucia shouted, "You want to stink of a sewer and show us all once again how lacking you are, I will not be blamed for it. *Dios mio*, these dresses are ghastly! Is this what I will be expected to wear here? Split skirts? Never! How much more of a burden could you be? We came here for the best life might offer, and *you* are the reason we cannot enjoy it." As if she did not care to be overheard, the woman muttered, "The first time I am allowed to leave my apartments in days and *this* is all I'm afforded. And the clothes, I have been ordered to cover my body from neck to toes, thanks to your preferences in fashion. My entire mating wardrobe is forbidden."

Ignoring the woman's ramblings, Brenya slipped from damp sheets and padded to the window. No hand reached out to test the door. No thoughts of taking the golden fork and fleeing for her freedom arrived. Her attention was on the rising moon; the way light cast from its beautiful face was slightly bent by the shape of the Dome.

It led an eerie light over a city that did not glitter as it should have in the dark.

Because she had been caught…

Lockdown had been engaged.

There would be barriers bolted into place that could not be opened with a golden fork and knife.

The Commodore had anticipated she would run, but Annette had been right. There was nowhere to run.

Not through the city she loved. Not to sandy beaches

she'd flown over on her ill-fated way to Thólos. Not to the ruins of the once great Paris.

The Alpha was hooked into her chest, raging like a roaring lion. The entirety of the city had been shut down.

Annette's child was probably being smothered in that moment.

It was over.

Lucia returned, beautiful and lithe, her arms full of fresh frothy white material, and watching her reflection in the window, Brenya couldn't find it in her to hate the female. The foreign Omega had said it herself—she had come here for *the best life*. Being mated to Ancil would be the worst.

Though Lucia clearly didn't understand that yet.

"Did he tell you he will murder his son? Annette's life will be next."

Compunction soured an angry expression to one of discomfiture. "No. But I will not lie and pretend that such an outcome has not occurred to me. The customs and laws regarding Omegas in this Dome are centuries behind the progress of Greth. I cannot be expected to change them overnight, especially when our Commmodorina does nothing with her influence. You have done nothing for any of us—your Omega guests locked away for these past weeks? We have not been able to even speak with one another. But, why should you concern yourself with your kind? You lay in filth and refuse to wash yourself."

There was only one thing Brenya might offer. "I will request that Jacques send you my honey."

Confused, Lucia cocked her head. "What does that even mean?"

Brenya turned away from the view. "It means I can do nothing for you."

"You could take a bath."

She could. Brenya could do this one and only thing for the woman who had inadvertently led to the destruction of two innocents. "It will be the only thing I ever do for you, Lucia."

"Fair enough." Setting the fresh gown on a nearby divan, Lucia tossed her sheet of shining black hair. "And know this. At no time did I suggest we be friends."

"That is good. The Commodore has tortured all my friends."

It was as if the female was finally starting to understand. Painted lips parted as if she might speak, but only silence grew between them. Turning from the view of a city she loved, Brenya went to the lavatory and stepped down into the steaming tub.

The water was warm, a comfort. The company was anything but.

18

Despite her acerbic jabs, Lucia had taken great pains in assuring Brenya was scrubbed clean, patted dry with soft towels, her hair wrung out and dried with a moisture transfer unit. It was then combed into order.

Chastising Brenya for failing to take care of her mottled skin, the Omega went so far as to dig through Jacques' cabinets in search of bandages and unguent.

Chin pinched in between the woman's pointed, lacquered nails, Brenya allowed Lucia to turn her head and expose the wound that refused to heal.

One glance, and the foreigner said, "This is infected."

Brenya didn't care and said as much.

A light smack came to her cheek, Lucia turning up her nose. "You should care. You will be judged on this mark for the rest of your life. It will be captured in paintings and projections. Talked about by an entire civilization throughout their history, and there is already the unfortunate issue of your face."

"How I look doesn't matter. Omegas are meant to be people." And really, what was the point of beauty? It didn't do anything. Just as disfigurement had done nothing. Jacques knotted her either way.

With a mean laugh, Lucia chided her. "Whoever told you that lie has never lived as an Omega. I have five older sisters, all Omegas. To be one of us is to be always at war. With each other, with ourselves, all the while working hard to impress the Alphas. Do not think I say this to be cruel. Both my nose and eyes were improved so I might outshine rivals." All of this was said as those sharp nails began to poke at the open, oozing wound. "There is an abscess that needs to be drained."

No warning was offered to brace for the pain; Lucia just pinched the flesh of Brenya's throat until an audible pop proceeded a stinking flow of puss. Despite the short-lived agony, instant relief followed, whatever needed purging drained, damaged skin sinking in on itself.

"Green." Shaking her head as if blood and gore was nothing but another inconvenience, Lucia swabbed up and sanitized the mess. Next came unguent, followed by a large gauze patch, taped down so quickly it was obvious Lucia had training in such things. "It was poor taste for the Commodore to bite you twice when the first one was well-placed and in proportion to your neck and shoulder— exactly where gowns could be cut to highlight the claiming mark. For such a glamourous city, the men are a bit savage, aren't they? That is what happens when there are no proper women available to tame their urges and keep them in line."

Keep them in line? With what, a cattle prod?

Despite the tangle of her insides, the hurt of her outsides, and the sure feeling that all of this was a waste of time, Brenya found it in her to offer a single dry chuckle.

"You will see."

Doubtful. After all, she was going to be judged for trying to free Jules Havel. And she already judged herself deeply for failing Annette again.

The loud, endlessly talking Lucia kept up a constant vocal stream of her every thought while simultaneously bandaging and dressing a woman who had no interest in responding.

But the work had been done, and done quickly—another heavy, uncomfortable dress hung from a shoulder that was swelling under the fabric. Kissing a throat that was oozing infection into a bandage.

A loud squawk from Lucia and Alpha guards swarmed the room. Brenya was surrounded by no less than eight prime Alphas, encased as they quickly ushered the pair of women down the halls. At her side, Lucia had no trouble with managing her skirts in the hurried gait; she didn't struggle as Brenya did to keep all the fabric from twisting around her feet. She looked regal, bright-eyed.

While Brenya was panting with exhaustion at the pace. While she could hardly breathe for the stiffness of the fabric at her neck and the added weight of a diamond collar that dripped like starlight over her shoulders and chest.

She needed to catch her breath, already snapped at for wiping sweat from her forehead and mussing the twisted configuration of her hair.

"You don't have time to be lazy, Commodorina. Curl up and complain later."

The statement was so far off base that it was almost impossible for Brenya not to tear at the style of her hair and set her stinging roots free, or yank off the diamonds dripping from her neck.

She'd had enough!

If Jacques wanted to punish her for doing what was best for the Dome, then he could come do so right there in the hall. What was coming for her didn't require such fuss or pretension.

Let those who feed off her people see her as she was.

Brenya dug in her heels, the entire party surrounding her stopping so abruptly Lucia almost ran into the guard running point.

A new side of the aggressive Omega appeared. Lucia went from exacerbated to nervous. "What are you doing? I told you there is no time."

Sucking in a deep breath to answer, Brenya froze.

Was that ozone?

Smoke?

The very quintessential signs of an electrical fire. And why were there so many guards and workers shuffling around the hall to her right?

There had been a fire, not a meter away from where she stood, Brenya having been so self-possessed that she had not noticed the char marks.

That was unacceptable. Her basic duty was to notice the minutia so unseen issues could be attended to before they became dangerous problems.

Lucia took her arm, urging her forward. "There is no time for you to stop and look at the scenery."

Brushing away the woman's touch, Brenya grabbed a handful of skirt, hefting it high so she could actually move in the ugly dress, and went straight to the char marks on the far wall.

Whispering to herself, she said, "This shouldn't be here."

She had not even come this way. Furthermore, sorting through the memories of the night, Brenya could recall no action that would have triggered a voltage surge. She had purposefully avoided all electrical conduits so as not to trigger any alarms.

Behind her, Lucia demanded of the silent guards, "Why is she staring at the wall like that?"

Having been intimate with several of the palace's maintenance shafts, Brenya was certain that the well-maintained circuitry did not experience random surges of this nature. Even the shafts themselves were spotless—worthy of Palo Corps's mark of excellence.

An impatient hand came to Brenya's arm, Lucia barking, "What part of 'men of such status do not wait' did you not understand, Commodorina?"

Still studying the pattern of the char marks on the wallpaper about the light fixture before her, Brenya said, "*Commodorina* is not a word in our language. I understand that you are attempting to give me a designation, but I do not have one anymore."

"You need a title. What else would I call you? Brenya? That is too familiar for the mate of a king. Next, you'd expect me to allow servants to call me Lucia."

Distracted, calculating the why of what was before her, Brenya muttered to the distraction, "He's not a king."

Speaking of the *not king*...

"Brenya!" The name was shouted with a bite, sailing down the halls as if Jacques had cracked a whip toward the entire party for insolence.

Raging as he rushed, physically puffed up and eyes threatening murder, the Commodore roared, "You were ordered to escort my mate immediately to me, under the highest level of security. And I find you loitering in the halls!"

Standing at attention, the guard standing point said, "Sir, our orders expressly state that we may not touch or speak to Brenya Perin unless her life is in imminent peril."

"*It is!*" Viciously, Jacques Bernard shoved the armed Alpha aside. As the guard careened off the wall, the Commodore made a rough grab at Brenya's arm.

She had witnessed Jacques in various terrifying states, but she had never seen him like this.

The physical effect was inescapable. Eyes wide, she backed away.

Or tried to. He had her so tightly there was nothing to do

but swallow her racing heart and try to keep up as he outpaced the party.

When her feet caught on her skirts, he dragged her, practically ripping her arm from the socket.

Behind them, the guards and a suddenly silent Lucia trailed.

Once the racing party reached a door flanked by further security, Jacques pulled Brenya around so he might take account of the panting, startled woman in his grip.

It was only then it seemed to occur to him that he was hurting her and that she could hardly breathe.

His grip on her arm altered from cruel to gently kneading. As if he might chase away what smarted. As if he wanted to offer her comfort.

Drinking down her wide-eyed expression, he quickly smoothed her hair back into place with an expertise that outweighed that of Lucia.

Accent heavy, the Omega interjected, "Great Commodore, she refused cosmetics."

Snarling at the interruption, the Commodore turned his attention from Brenya to the supplicating Omega. He measured the woman with her eyes demurely turned to the floor, her head at a subtle bow. "You have done well enough, I suppose, Lucia." Addressing the guard at Lucia's side, Jacques barked an order. "Escort this woman to the security chief's residence. Lock her in."

If there was any disappointment having her short-lived freedom stripped away, Lucia did not betray it. She curtseyed, and she obeyed.

In a much softer tone, Jacques blended a purr into his words. "Brenya, I need you to catch your breath for me. When you walk into this room, you will walk in as a queen. Remember that you represent every life under this Dome. That you have made an oath to them. I caution you to choose your words well, and think of how much you love..." It seemed as if he was going to say "me," but the Alpha hesitated and offered, "your people," instead.

The violence, the rushing, the lack of sleep, Brenya's failure to free Jules Havel or see Annette and her baby safe, the disappointment and the regret... the entire night was impacting her ability to think straight.

Worse was the anxiety tolling through the pair-bond. *His anxiety*. It pinged about her throat, weaving itself into her confusion... because he didn't seem angry with her.

The way he was petting and fretting, how he obsessively touched her face.

He seemed afraid *for* her.

And he was still fidgeting with her clothing and organizing her hair just so, tucking loose strands behind her unpierced ears—forcing her necklace to lay flat where prongs had snagged the lace across her chest.

Cupping her cheeks, Jacques urged her to meet his gaze. "You look like a queen. Beautiful. Everything any man might desire in a mate."

Blinking, unsure what to say, because none of this made sense, she felt him place a soft kiss on her mouth. It lingered, followed by another on her forehead, before he tucked her into his elbow and ordered the doors to be opened.

The small, plain room was crowded, yet heavy silence waited.

All this fuss for nothing but a cramped COM room?

Ancil was there, scowling. The set of his ticking jaw a clear threat. Other faces were familiar to her, Brenya having seen the men at the state dinner. The tense crowd each wore an embroidered coat; each had whatever hair they grew on their heads caught in a tight braid. All of them stared at her. Expectation, judgment, dislike, intrigue.

Brenya had nothing for them. No explanation. No apology.

They deserved nothing from her.

So her attention went elsewhere as Jacques led her to the center of the tight space. She observed communications panels far more advanced than any she'd ever seen. The layout of the instruments was complex, the interconnected workings of the machines outside her forte.

These weren't like the glorious interworking of a clock. They were not engineering marvels. They were outside of her scope and training. Nothing like the controls of the ship she had stolen, there was no intuitive understanding of what those knobs and consoles might do.

It seemed a strange room for judgment and pomp.

A man cleared his throat. At her side, Jacques tensed in response.

Odd.

Yet it stole her attention away from the communications panel.

"Good evening, Brenya."

That voice did not belong in that place with those people.

It certainly didn't need to affect courtesy, as if the Beta who'd spoken possessed any measure of kindness.

Blood running cold at the sight of Ambassador Jules Havel politely nodding her way, Brenya refused to play whatever game this was. Voice cutting, she let him know exactly how she felt. "It is not a good evening."

It had been one of the worst evenings.

How he had gone from starved, unwashed prisoner who'd had nothing but a bucket to relieve himself in, to a polished and finely dressed free man who appeared to command the room did not compute.

Looking upon him, knowing that he did not forgive, that his bitterness cost Annette and her child a chance for life, she saw nothing but a living amalgamation of her disappointment with the world. And Brenya let him know it when honey eyes met shocking blue.

With a dip of his head, it seemed the Ambassador agreed. "I know you are tired, and I concede that you are correct. It has not been a good evening *for some*."

"That is enough, Ambassador," Jacques growled in warning. "Brenya Perin has been brought as was requested."

Smirking, Jules stared right at her. The unwavering void of him yawning open, as if he mentally flicked a finger for her to approach.

She did not.

Rooted, she stared right back at him, seeing all the way right into the emptiness of such a man.

It was from that place he spoke, honest in his evil. "Specific events of the evening, and fruitless attempts at negotiation by the leadership of Bernard Dome, have done nothing to spare you this moment."

"I never asked you to spare *me*." She had asked him to save Annette and her baby. "I begged you to spare my people. I offered—"

"Be quiet." It was as if his order had come from inside her and not from the male's lips. She jerked back from the force of it, pulling at the collar of her dress as if he'd stolen her breath.

Turning his horrible, burning gaze away, Ambassador Jules Havel spoke to the screens. "Chancellor Shepherd of Greth Dome, husband to Queen Svana, may I introduce my mate."

How had Brenya not noticed what waited on the screens? Their display of a massive male practically blotting out the sun behind him. That there shouldn't even be sun, because it was the middle of the night. That the insignia on the wall was in a language Brenya could not read, and that the man himself had similar black marks edging from his collar and up his neck as one Jules Havel.

She knew who this was. Titles meant nothing. Four words were enough to name him. "You destroyed Thólos Dome."

Though his projection towered over the party due to the height of the screens, Brenya was certain he would tower over them in person as well. And he seemed pleased with her statement, though it didn't show in his reaction. It was in the way he held her gaze—that he allowed her the time to look upon him and absorb all that could be measured from a projection. That she might memorize the color of the walls behind him. The simple lines of a functional desk so unlike the filigreed furnishings of Central. There was a lack of embellishment or ornamentation in the man's clothes.

He wore a gold band on his finger.

The men packed and loudly breathing in the room looked ridiculous in comparison: powdered and painted and dripping with shiny things.

Fingers still hooked in her collar so she might take a full breath, Brenya understood at last why she had been brought here. "I stole your ship, abducted your Ambassador, and attempted to fly to Thólos. Once there, I intended to make repairs on the Dome."

The man on the monitor, his voice impressively deep, lacking all melody yet interesting on the ear, spoke. "Why?"

Such a simple question with such complicated answers. Swallowing, sad, Brenya said, "Because I had yet to understand that there is nowhere to run."

As if the response were satisfactory, the Chancellor across the world scowled at the Alpha standing at her side. "Step away from her, Jacques Bernard. I will confer with the mate of Jules Havel without your interference."

19

To Brenya's utter astonishment, Jacques obeyed an order from a male oceans away. Low warning growl emanating from the Alpha at her side—the male aggressive in both posture and scent—gently untucking her fingers from his arm, he gave her a lingering look. One Brenya did not return.

Her attention was solely focused on the man who could command a Commodore.

This *Shepherd* stared at her with the same acute attention.

This man who Jacques confessed he could not defeat in war.

Which in itself was a bizarre concept.

Brenya had not put much consideration into the whispers Jacques lavished on her ear when she was under him. There had been greater concerns to address since she'd woken with her head split open for two relative strangers to pick through.

Staring, Brenya had already cataloged every last exposed scar on this Shepherd's flesh, noted that his hair fell at altering angles. Patches of skin had been torn from his skull, upsetting the pattern of growth. His knuckles were ragged from repeated breaks and no doubt ached deep in the bone.

His nose had been damaged on more than one occasion.

Shepherd's lips—like the pulled flesh under her eye—did not lay properly. His top lip dragged upward. But unlike her own face, Brenya did not imagine people would consider his imperfection a disfigurement.

Leaning his mass closer to the camera, Shepherd said, "You are not afraid of me."

Maybe she should be, but she wasn't. Not that she didn't comprehend that her next breath was in this man's worn hands. As Lucia said, Brenya had been brought here to be judged. Just not for the crime she had assumed.

Standing in the center of a crowded COM room, dressed in white that contrasted the black walls of a work zone. Men at her back, at her side, staring with scorn, entreating, smelling, ruining the air of the room with their blended *loud* stench.

The Ambassador, dressed in black, the simplicity of his clothing a beacon in a room of artifice and glitter, came to stand at her side.

Stealing the space that had been Jacques' only moments before, he addressed the man across the seas. "She is not afraid of you."

Maneuvering whatever it was that made up a pair-bond—an attachment that didn't belong to him, that should not have existed at all—the Ambassador's statement only disclosed a fraction of her thoughts. She was plenty afraid: for Annette, for the baby, for the friend whose name was not permitted to pass her lips.

Whatever Thólos had done to earn this man's temper, Brenya would not see it done in Bernard Dome. Not because of her mistakes. "I am responsible for the situation regarding Ambassador Jules Havel. I did not know he was on the shi—"

The Alpha on the screen interrupted. "Do you understand what a pair-bond entails?"

No. "In theory. It has been described to me as something that would help me find happiness in what it means to be Omega. The moment it was forged was painful, and I have had little time to navigate the mental...." Brenya could not find a word. What did her opinion on a pair-bond matter anyway? "As I was saying, if I had not stolen Jules Havel's ship, he would not be *inside me*. Nor should he be. Your Ambassador should be free to return home." There was really no other way to put it.

Had her voice just wavered? Why was it so hot in that room?

A brush of another's hand came to the back of Brenya's fingers. A reminder that the man she had harmed stood at her side, that he was watching her in place of acknowledging the man.

The warmth in the room, the only scent that was not laced with tension, came from him.

Gathering up her fingers as if it were normal for them to touch, Jules held them tight.

As if he had not just mocked her when she'd come to save him. As if he had not refused to help good people leave a bad place.

Behind them, Jacques growled, he cursed, yet he didn't step forward and tear them apart.

Brenya found then that her eyes had moved to where her fingers intertwined with a stranger's, that she was confused at the fact that something so simple offered comfort. A man who had promised to hurt her.

It was clear who held all the power in the room. It wasn't the Alpha on the screen, it was the Beta silently urging her to meet his poisonous gaze.

Eyes should not be that shade of blue.

"You were kind to me on the ship when I was frightened. You offered explanations no one else had. You kept your distance when I was, um…"

Jules, his voice deep and smooth as a flowing river, said, "In your first estrous, Brenya Perin."

Cheeks red from shame, she nodded.

"The men of Bernard Dome do not understand what took place that day any better than you do. Through a stupid act of pride, in manipulating an experience that can never be undone, they have earned an enemy. And no, Brenya Perin, I will not grant them mercy. But I will demand that you understand that the consequence these men must face is not because you stole my ship when you thought to escape an abusive Alpha. It is not because you were ignorant of the situation in Thólos and the agreement between two governments that no aid might be offered to survivors of that fallen Dome."

Soft threats in gentle words, no emotion or mental signal. A clear threat.

Because she was correct. No pair-bond would keep this man from hurting her.

Everyone was watching her, because whatever happened in this room hinged upon her completely. He was still holding her hand in both of his, and now she understood the gesture. It wasn't comfort; it was control.

Of Jacques Bernard who could do nothing to prevent the Beta from touching her, though he seethed through the link.

Facing him fully to say what no male in the room had dared, she laid her free hand atop his grip and said what they had left to her. "Jules, what was done to you was wrong, and I am sorry for my part in it. I thought I could make it right, and I don't truly understand what to offer or how to undo it. Teach me how, and I will try. But if you attempt to hurt my people, I will kill you."

"Ms. Perin," the man on the monitor with a voice of coarse rocks and scars called. "A moment of your time, please."

She would not have looked at him, not as she waited for Jules to address a threat from a woman he understood was capable of things no one else in that room might grasp. Yet Jules pulled one of his hands from between hers and lay a finger to the side of her chin so Brenya might break their extended stare and turn her attention to the looming Shepherd.

He was still watching her in that way of his. The same way she watched.

Unblinking.

"Five men in Central died tonight from Red Consumption. I released the virus into Bernard Dome in response to your government's treatment of my Ambassador and failure to uphold our agreement regarding the exchange of Omegas for orange trees."

That was why the city was in lockdown! It wasn't because she'd been caught. In fact, neither Jules nor Shepherd had informed the leadership of Bernard Dome of what she'd tried to do.

Why?

Holding tighter to Jules Havel's hand as if he might give her strength instead of pain, Brenya shook her head. Because the things she was hearing could not be true.

Shepherd continued, "It was a controlled release, fully contained—the virus has been destroyed by incineration protocol and will not spread from that location. So understand that the day Jules Havel dies, so too will every last soul in your Dome choke to death on their blood. Be cautious of your threats."

The screen changed to display an accelerated recording of five horrible, choking deaths, the bodies left lying in their fluids for ages before a delayed incineration protocol began. The camera burned, and the story ended. The story was so much more than the deaths. It was the very terrifying fact that a terrorist who had already destroyed one Dome for reasons she didn't know, had conquered another, and now had power over hers.

She didn't even know why she said it, the words small. "I have never seen anyone die."

"So long as Jules Havel thrives, you will not see it again."

All Brenya could think of was the Beta servant on the screen who had done nothing but her duty. How she had reached out for help and the men had ignored her. How her death would be explained away as reassignment.

Not one of her sisters in Beta Sector would know to mourn her.

Tears spilling, Brenya freed her hand from the Beta's and gave her back to Chancellor Shepherd to snarl at Jacques Bernard—a full, threatening growl that would have seen her aggressively raped were Jacques in the situation to punish her. "You told me that the Bernard Dome could not defeat the leader of Greth! Yet you thought to *leash a rabid dog* as if there would be no consequence. You said Jules Havel could never hurt me, while *you* were hurting me. You forced both him and myself into a pair-bond only you desired. You starved and imprisoned a person you described as a terrorist. A man who had already destroyed an entire civilization. Jacques Bernard, this is your fault! You allowed dangerous men inside my home for OMEGAS! For sex! Every one of you in this room is the reason that Beta on the screen died terrified, away from her sisters. Your greed."

Spinning so sharply her skirts flared, Brenya faced down the staring man on the screen. "And as for you, Chancellor

Shepherd. Whatever took place in Thólos, it is not the situation in Bernard Dome. Do not judge my people by the actions of the few bad men. Unlike the corruption of Central, Alpha and Beta sectors are populated by good, hardworking innocents. Who were conditioned, just like I was, to serve one another for the greater good. Murdering that Beta female was *wrong*."

"That is the nature of war, Ms. Perin. Innocents always pay."

So be it. "Then I will pay. What is it that you want?"

"Orange trees for my bride. And as Jules Havel has chosen to remain in Bernard Dome so you might survive your unnatural pair-bond, a hostage in exchange."

It was the second time the Chancellor had mentioned orange trees, yet it was the first time anyone mentioned that Jules leaving would equate to her inability to survive an *unnatural* pair-bond.

"Yes, Brenya. Shepherd is telling you that if I return to Greth, you will die."

Irritated she had to even say it aloud, Brenya grit her teeth. "Then I die. Go home to your Rebecca."

"I have no Rebecca. My wife died in Thólos. As did our two sons." How could anyone say so horrible a thing with so little passion? How could a man breathe when he was totally dead inside?

A slow blink, shunting her eyes closed, Brenya drew in a deep breath. Pursing her lips on an exhale, she knew better than to trust. This demand for an exchange was too convenient.

Jules already knew what she'd ask for. So did Shepherd.

They had all been conversing long before she had come into the room.

It couldn't be this easy. *Nothing* could be this easy. Jules Havel was going to claim a price from her later—a great one—as Brenya was going to overreach. "Annette, First wife of Ancil, Security Chief of Bernard Dome, and her newborn son, Matthieu. They will go to Greth."

Ancil was already shouting in outrage, pushing his weight forward yet bodily restrained by the Alphas at his side.

But Brenya was not finished. She looked Shepherd dead in the eye. "As Jules has chosen to continue his residence in Bernard, you will need a pilot to deliver your orange trees and new citizens. My former tech, George Gerard, will fly your ship and remain in Greth as well."

It was Jacques' turn to rage, though unlike Ancil, no one dared attempt to hold him back. Rushing forward to address Chancellor Shepherd, he barked, "I do not agree with the release of George Gerard. I will provide another to pilot the ship."

"Jules, the queen sends her regards to your mate. Ms. Perin," Shepherd said, ignoring Jacques' bluster and pomp, "I believe you will be a worthy match for my brother."

The screen went dark, those men who had not been previously shouting joining in the melee. So much noise in so small a room, yet Brenya ignored it. Just as she ignored the hands of an Alpha shaking her, as she ignored her name being shouted in her ear.

Cerulean eyes fringed by dark lashes glowed with a life

that might only belong to the dead. His lips parted, and his price was claimed. "Your keeping and all rights to you now belong to me."

Snarling, a hand taller than the Beta, Jacques pushed Brenya bodily behind him. "That was not what we agreed!"

As if no immediate threat to Jules' safety snarled and spat, Jules offered a calm and even, "Monsieur Carlin, please escort my bride to our new quarters. Jacques, you may accompany her and explain the contract you signed before the members of parliament in this room. At no time will Ms. Perin be left alone with you. Should I find her soiled before I might consummate the marriage, I will have your testicles removed."

Red-faced, spittle flying, Jacques roared, "You think you are the first challenger I have had for my position? You reach too far. The Dome will not back a foreign Beta usurper."

Unmoved, unflinching, Jules Havel made his position clear. "I believe it appropriate that you refer to me as Commodore."

20

The room was overly crowded, which clearly agitated his Omega. Hovering near, so his shape might blot out the members of parliament who had escorted them to the Red Room, so Brenya might stop glaring at Ancil, Jacques pressed a kiss to her hair.

"*Mon chou*, I want you to remember what we shared tonight." Feverish lips at her ear, Jacques Bernard whispered so no other *traitorous* present member of parliament might hear. "I can feel you shaking. Please, my love, don't be afraid. Hush now."

His mate didn't answer, worrying her lip as her doe eyes jumped from one part of his dead brother's apartments to another.

Jacques hated this room. Everything was in shades of red. Ironically fitting, considering the amount of blood that had spilled from the windbag when Jacques had torn him apart for the title of Commodore.

With his last brother dead, Jacques had chosen new apartments, breaking with tradition by rejecting the room of all those who had come before him. His right as Commodore. A new, glorious era for Bernard Dome.

Under his rule, all had thrived.

Fitting that a foreign rebel who had the audacity to assume a title meant power would want to sleep in the quarters of a bygone era.

It meant nothing!

Bernard Dome knew who owned them. They knew who to thank for what they had, the luxuries they had indulged in, the pussy, the anus, the throat.

All orders came from Jacques Bernard—even the order for this illusory transfer in power.

And he had been good to his people. Generous to Parliament.

He knew how every last member liked to fuck, who they wanted in their beds, traded their daughters to their sons in advantageous matches that conserved power. He'd inundated them with the prettiest Beta servants and made sure disease was unable to spread at any of the elite brothels.

Even their wives had been serviced with treats, parties, gifts. Many of them, he had fucked personally when they had batted their eyelashes his way.

They would remember that when this new Beta tried to tempt them with platitudes they didn't want.

All Central wanted was Omegas.

Omegas Jacques had already begun acquiring and having trained. Pure Bernard stock that would be conditioned for those he had handpicked to receive.

Clean slates like Brenya, these females could be taught to please in ways the uppity foreign Omegas turned their nose up at.

When Ancil had groused that Lucia refused anal sex, Jacques had laughed. And then he had shown his life-long friend and rival a projection of how he had taken Brenya's ass in the bath only hours after sealing the pair-bond.

That was how an Alpha commanded his mate.

Damn the red room, damn the Beta Ambassador, damn Chancellor Shepherd. Damn them all!

His *mon chou* would be back in his bed and out of that hideous room. She would be ensconced and safe as he nurtured her into her purpose.

Back in his arms, back with her lips stretched around his dick. Cock hard with the need to scent her—hating that she had bathed, his leavings washed away—he dripped against his trousers. The air filled with his spice, with an enticement only an Alpha could provide to an Omega.

What did this Beta charlatan think he could possibly do with an Omega pussy? It was hysterically ridiculous. The man could not even knot. How was she to know pleasure?

Petting his darling Brenya, trying his best to soothe, Jacques murmured, "Just… relax and think of me. It will be over quickly. And then he is to assure you are properly tended by your Alpha, the marriage contract was exceedingly clear. This is only a minor, *and short-lived*, inconvenience."

Struggling to contain his indignation, preparing to leave his mate in the hands of a *Beta*, Jacques straightened so she might see all of him.

How he strained at his pants for her. How he was still her Alpha. How she was still his darling.

Aching with the need to drive into her, he stroked his shaft through the fabric. From base to tip, flooding out globs of cream that already had her pupils dilating.

"You were ordered to leave her untainted, Jacques. I'd rather not suffer through watching another of my brothers die tonight."

Curling his lip at the low-level snot who dared call him anything other than Commodore, Jacques snarled, "You and I will have words over this insolence later."

The man's name was added to the growing tally of parliament members Jacques would personally murder that night. He'd kill their families too, their children… wipe their lineage from the face of the planet!

How dare these Alphas turn on him before he might explain that the satellites could all be shut down. Bernard Dome could retreat into itself for a safe eternity. Greth would be blind. Jules Havel would be restricted and tortured until there was an accounting of every potential location for whatever device had been used to release Red Consumption.

Already, sweeps were going out through the entire Dome for anything that looked out of place or stank of foreign sweat.

Fear had led weak men to make foolish choices.

With Ancil by his side, their position and control would be reinstated in a week.

The meek woman sitting on the edge of a blood-red bed would be home, and safe, and he would help her forget every last moment spent spread under the Beta fiend.

"I love you, *mon chou*."

The essence of her receded, only to come back crashing. Over and over, so caught in her own riptide, Jacques could not fully grasp the direction of her feelings.

Only that she was… grieving.

And that she had not heard a word he had said.

Understandable, considering the mutt thought he might actually pry him from his mate. A man who could have been drenched in trained pussy day and night for the rest of his life. Who would have lived in greater luxury than the *Red Rooms*.

"Do you want me to," pressing sweet kisses to her hair, he purred, "help you get excited?"

Robotic. His innocent Omega always sounded robotic when she was truly upset. "I want you to tell me the designation and name of the Beta female who died."

"I will… have this information by the time you are returned to me." It would be easy enough to scan the schedules of Betas chosen for brothel labor. In fact, Jacques was fairly sure he had ridden her on more than one occasion.

But all the females seemed to run together when one had tasted them all.

Tugging at the collar of her dress, his darling Brenya

stared forward and asked, "Do you know the identities of the men?"

Of course he did. He knew every last detail of every Alpha under the Dome not subjected to pharmaceutical control. "Yes. I knew them personally. Three of the four held seats in Parliament."

Ancil, pacing at his back, snarled. "An order has arrived for us to return to our quarters... *like peasants*. The ship is in the air, my traitorous cunt of a wife has taken the child. And your Omega's lover is managing the controls with no issue."

Brenya's shoulders fell from her ears, honey eyes finally focused. Right on Ancil. "No matter what life Annette and your son find in Greth, they will still have one. Someday, he will be old enough to return and take everything that is yours."

"SILENCE YOUR FUCKING BITCH!"

Facing his friend with an expression that sent the rest of the males scuttling away, Jacques lifted a hand to warn Ancil that such outbursts would not be tolerated.

But the Omega egged on the dangerous man. "And by the time he comes back, you will have withered. You will be too old to so much as meet the eye of the son you never met yet intended to murder. I don't imagine your firstborn will have much mercy for you either."

It was so fast, Jacques could not anticipate the blow. His lifelong friend struck his fragile mate hard enough that she fell back against the blood-red coverlet.

The scent of Omega blood in the air, and Jacques became a mindless beast intent on the sound of breaking bone.

Having trained for years with this male, he knew where to strike for maximum damage. As did his adversary. They rolled in a vicious tangle of strikes and snarls.

Though Ancil was assuredly dangerous, he was not in the bloodlust that fueled a male protecting his mate. Jacques broke his wrists, an elbow, a shoulder. No quarter for a man he had known since the cradle.

Purging the ichor of so terrible a night, Jacques continued to rend. To not only crush an enemy but to show all who observed why he had earned the title Commodore.

Strips were torn from the face of his friend, disfiguring beauty while Ancil whined for mercy.

The supplication was too late. Jacques would not even hear him beg, preferring the gagged sounds of a man who had lost the ability to control that passage of air into his body.

Together, they had lost the influence of their positions. They had lost treasured possessions.

Together, they could have reclaimed the Dome.

Now, Jacques would do it alone.

With Ancil's neck compressed between his bicep and forearm, Jacques toyed with his prey, licking at his friend's bloody ear in a reminder that when they were younger, they had played this way—the winner of the match fucking what he had subdued, as per the rules of the game.

Those days, Jacques had enjoyed the spoils.

Both of the males had always enjoyed it.

An atrocious shade of crimson, the flesh of his cheek hanging loose, Ancil began to lose consciousness.

But that was not the way an ingrate would be led to death.

Releasing Ancil to parquet floors—lacquered, as legend would say, with the blood of those who opposed the first Commodore of Bernard Dome—the defeated Alpha began to stir.

"How many times did I warn you to keep your hands and eyes to yourself regarding my mate?"

A tooth missing, mouth bleeding, Ancil struggled to say, "Peace, brother."

"Did I not give you everything you desired?" Turning to face down the scattered men in the room, Jacques shouted, "Did I not give you all your every last whim?"

Stifled murmurs and stiff nods were offered by a few. Others, wisely keeping their eyes averted.

"Witness what I do to traitors!"

His foot came crashing down on Ancil's neck with such force it cracked far more than bone. The stained floor, as old as the Dome itself, split beneath his heel. Ancil's running blood swallowed deep enough between the floorboards that the red of the room no longer struck Jacques as garish.

It was exactly as it should be. A place for enemies to die.

So he silently vowed, meeting the eyes of his reeling mate, that it would be in this room that Jacques fed the blood of Jules Havel to the Dome.

Three floors down, an Omega screamed.

∼

Quite a fuss had been made over her face once Ancil lay in a heap of protruding bones and blood.

"I don't think her cheek is broken, but... a physician should be called to mend where her skin split along her scar."

A raging Alpha roared, "Stand away from my mate!"

Woozy, Brenya held her finger to her face, unsure if the slippery red had come from her or from Ancil as he'd screamed for mercy.

The crowd was growing tighter, jostling bodies pulling her to and fro to see the damage. There was too much touching. Too much noise. Too much everything. "Don't touch me!"

Like magic, all backed off save one.

The same older gentleman who had spoken to her at the state dinner, the one who had stood beside Ambassador Jules, bowed. "Madam, you need a physician, and the Commodore will need to be notified that you were wounded."

Silent despite the age of the creaking floors, Jules stalked straight to where Brenya braced against the bed. Looking only at her, he addressed the Alpha who thought to stand in the way. "You had an hour in which to explain that you'd sold your mate to me for skin on your back, and instead, I find Brenya Perin bleeding and the Security Advisor dead."

Bloody hand to his chest, Jacques faced down another man, heaving with the breath of an Alpha ready to kill.

"Control yourself, Jacques." The *new Commodore*, Jules Havel, was still looking only at her, yet addressing a very serious threat as if Jacques were nothing but a gnat. "So much as look at me in a way I dislike and see what I do."

It was hard to look away from such an intense stare, from a face that showed nothing, from a man who was as empty as she was full, but she did. Honey eyes darted to see Jacques offer a stiff bow.

Taking her chin, Jules studied the damage while addressing all onlookers. "Take the carcass and leave. Jacques Bernard will not get what we agreed to until I claim what I desire."

Chilled by the coldness of such a statement, Brenya took her face from Jules' touch, turning away from both males.

The room cleared.

Jacques had left her.

Blood smeared from the spot where Ancil had died at her feet all the way to the door. No one had even thought to wipe it away.

The Beta certainly didn't; he just continued to stare until a knock came to the door. The unexpected sound left her jumping, squeaking out a noise that summed up exactly how she felt.

Small.

Apparently, one of the Alphas had indeed summoned a physician. One Brenya remembered from when she had first been dragged to Central, torn and in the midst of withdrawals.

The Beta noted her instant increase in anxiety, taking those too bright eyes from her face at last.

Addressing the physician bowing at the door, Jules offered an unaffected, "You are not needed. Leave your supplies and retreat."

The doors closed, two cases left on the bloodstained floor.

"The archives are well-kept in Bernard," the man said, moving toward the door to retrieve the physician's things. "This Red Room was designed to host the reigning Commodore. There are no access panels. The windows are practically unbreakable. Every piece of the design was constructed in such a way that the most paranoid of leaders might sleep with less concern they would be murdered for their title—yet the room was stained with blood. To remind them of the price of power. As you have noticed, there is no balcony and only one door. The guards outside that door have already received the updated registries. All of Alpha Sector is on alert, and Central is under their control."

She didn't care about the room or the fact that he claimed to have cornered her far better than Jacques might.

The man set the cases on the bed, rifling through their contents before snapping on gloves.

Wincing when he touched her face, Brenya closed her eyes and reminded herself to breathe.

"Had Jacques taken the time to pay attention to what was going on in your head, you would have been locked in this room ages ago."

The prick of a needle entered the swelling flesh of her check, a shock of stinging injection that left her trapping a groan in her throat.

Sweet numbness followed. Until he pricked a new spot, and then another.

When the pain subsided enough that Brenya might unclench her jaw, she answered, "I have always enjoyed the color red."

A hint of a smirk came to the man threading a curved needle with wire. "As have I."

The Bernard flag was red. Commendations came on red ribbons. That is where her mind went when the first stab of the needle pierced her flesh. Though painless, the tug and pull of suturing skin was unpleasant.

Yet, Jules Havel proceeded quickly, as if he had sewn skin to skin many times in the past. Knotting his second stitch, he asked, "What did Jacques whisper in your ear?"

"That I was to lay back… and think of him."

"What else?"

"That this would be a short-lived inconvenience."

With a dry laugh, the man began another suture. The hooked needle delved back into her skin, she continued to bleed.

Trying to remain still so he might continue, Brenya asked, "Will it be?"

"That depends on your definition of inconvenience." The final knot was tied. "You are my wife as of me stamping my claim as Commodore upon the contracts—"

"First wife," she corrected. If he was like Ancil, he could claim a Beta as well.

Finished assessing his work, those terrible eyes bore into hers. "I will not be taking another wife."

She had no response.

"I own you in the sense of Bernard law. But I possess you in the sense of your spirit, and I am disinterested in setting you free. Which means I cannot kill Jacques Bernard."

Five people had died of Red Consumption in her precious

home. Ancil had been slaughtered before her. Brenya could only sum up such a cold question to shock. "What happens if Jacques Bernard dies?"

His answer was direct and equally uninformative. "You will discover that for yourself the next time you see Lucia."

Outside the red room, the sun had begun to warm the sky, Brenya taking in what was an even more remarkable view while iodine was blotted on her cheek.

"Are there other injuries that I have not seen?"

Sighing, Brenya felt exhaustion roll over her so suddenly she lurched. "Nothing Lucia didn't already see to."

"It seems the nature of our pair-bond is more physical than those I have observed in the past. What you are feeling is the sensation of Jacques being sedated. I can't have him running wild, murdering my people in a tantrum over losing his favorite toy."

It was an apropos comparison. "He told me you would give me back after you were done."

That subtle smirk was back. "Did he?"

She needed this to be over so she might find a few hours of sleep;, otherwise, she was going to crack. "I would like to be excused from taking you down my throat until my cheek has healed. Kindly tell me, would you prefer that I brace on all fours. Or lay on my back. I was told earlier that I am expected to touch the male inside me, and I will strive to do so if that is what you wish."

Stripping off sterile gloves, Jules Havel commanded, "Take off your dress, Brenya Havel."

The name caught her even as her hands moved to reach

buttons she would not be able to unfasten without help. Once she processed that in less than a year she had gone from being 17C, to *mon chou*, to Brenya Perin, to Brenya Havel she found nothing but that damn necklace in the way.

Lowering her hands to her bloodstained lap, she confessed, "I cannot take this dress off by myself."

It should have registered sooner that he already stood between her legs. That he had been cradled there the entire time he had sewn the wound on her face—but the intimacy of the position only just sank in.

That was how tired she'd become.

Far too tired to resist when he reached around her neck to unclasp the necklace, Jules tossed it to the side as if it were nothing but rocks on a string. When he began on the buttons down her spine, she felt the fabric frill release her aching neck, and Brenya pulled in a full breath that was sweet with the scent of a hungry man.

Deft fingers undid one closure at a time until the gown parted and could be pulled from her shoulders. It was not her breasts he looked to when her dress pooled at her waist. It was the subtle swelling of her shoulders, the scratches from an Alpha who preferred to tear clothing from her skin, the fingerprints and bruises.

Each was inspected with naked fingers, her shoulder moved to test mobility, and scowled at when it was clear the tendon was inflamed.

"I have yet to see the footage of how you reached my cell, but once I have, I believe we are going to have a discussion about technique. This was an avoidable injury."

Insult brushed aside common sense. Brenya bit back, "I guarantee my climbing technique is far superior to yours, Jules Havel. I was climbing before I could walk."

"Hmm." He took a step back, surveying her torso in another sweep. "Stand and remove your skirt."

Silk and lace whispered to the ground, Brenya eager to be done with this.

"Turn."

She did, facing away while he brushed her hair from her back. His touch traced down her vertebrae, stopping on occasion for a thumb to dig in until she grunted. Yet each pass caused something tight to release.

Fingertips moved to her buttocks, gently pulling apart her flesh. She knew what he saw, why he asked, "How long ago did he do this?"

"Hours ago."

"Did you bleed?"

"No. He made sure I saw that I had not."

"I see." Physically turning her to face him, Jules met her eyes as he asked, "Any vaginal complaint?"

None that would impede whatever Jules Havel intended to do to her. "I was stretched with the pliarator earlier today. There should be nothing to prevent you from…"

"From what, Brenya Havel?"

The word was small. He made her feel small. "Penetration."

"Then climb into bed."

21

GRETH DOME

Despite her previous urges to deny Shepherd a proper nest, she built one around him as he snored. Nimbly arranging the wonderfully soft new things he'd provided. Gifts brought before he had come to her in need of comfort only a mate might provide. Claire created a wonder for him to wake in.

Since coming to Greth, she had never seen him so exhausted. Nor had there ever been a situation in which her subtle movements had not instantly jarred him from sleep. For crying out loud, she practically slept like a corpse so the Alpha would get the rest he so clearly needed.

But she refused to worry. Emotions could be controlled and explored later. Right now, she needed to take care of him.

So he could take care of everyone else.

Jules had a new wife now. Shepherd had shown Claire a

projection of a woman standing on a balcony, the wind dancing through her hair as she stared into the distance.

A scar dragged down one of the Omega's eyelids, puckered the flesh of her cheek.

An engaging scar on the face of an interesting woman.

Smiling at the picture, Claire told Shepherd she'd chosen a friend… so he could stop grousing.

"Brenya Havel does not speak your language, and she needs time, little one." Yet it was clear Shepherd was pleased by her declaration. "You come on strong, and the last year of her life has not been easy. Let's not overwhelm her."

"Then I will send a gift. A painting." She smiled, already knowing exactly which view of her garden to capture. "We can exchange letters."

It was so rare to catch Shepherd in an open act of contemplation. Which left Claire grinning as he looked to the side and pondered. "You could prepare for her your favorite Omega information."

"Omega information?" Chuckling before she nipped his chest, Claire hummed in the exact pitch that would make his eyes heavy. "Sure. I'll put together a manual."

It was meant to be a joke, but the way Shepherd looked at her…

"She was the first Omega in Bernard Dome in generations. It would be a kindness to give her some perspective."

Claire reeled, trying to imagine what life might have been like without a sisterhood of Omegas to guide her. A mother, Nona, all the women she had met with in secret because their lives required safety in numbers and vigilance.

"The Alpha who forged the bond. He hurt her," Claire whispered. Because of course he did. He wouldn't know what to do any more than Brenya might.

It was a situation that almost deserved pity for the male.

"A letter—some advice, from the wife of Jules' friend." Yawning, Shepherd finished with, "Articles you enjoy could be translated...."

Increasing the volume of her hum, Claire watched her mate's eyes close. Snores were instant.

His COM? She stole it. He could have it back after he slept more than three hours straight.

One of the most beautiful nests an Omega might create when their Alpha was already in it came to life. Claire, humming so loud she would be hoarse later.

He needed this.

The man had been away for almost two full days. She knew he had not slept, that his focus had been on the situation with Jules.

The sun rose, Claire tucked to the side of a sleeping giant. No tutors dared interrupt. Together, they dreamed until dusk.

She bathed. The time spent on her unruly hair... recognizing how badly she needed a trim. How long had it been since she'd cut her hair? Ends crunching between her fingertips, she frowned.

Thólos.

She could think of that place now without vomiting, not that it didn't sour her stomach all the same.

Making a mess of it, Claire tried to tidy up the split ends

by herself. Even with jagged edges, she looked in the mirror and saw something that mattered.

She saw herself.

Green eyes. Scars that would be covered by a pretty dress. Black hair. Pale skin. Cowardice.

"My name is Claire O'Donnell. I am the wife of Shepherd O'Donnell. Our son's name is Collin. And he would have been two this month."

Sucking in a deep breath, she looked herself in the eye and stated, "I am going to a movie. Everything will be okay."

When Shepherd woke, she was already in the kitchen. Trying out another concoction that might make his green sludge taste less like rotting garbage.

Smiling at a man with his hair sticking in every direction, Claire circled the counter to press a kiss to his lips. "Shepherd O'Donnell, would you like to take in a film with me tonight?"

The man's agitation… Claire was used to it. She even smirked when he accused, "You took my COM."

With obnoxiously wide eyes, Claire teased, "I called Dr. Osin and enacted *Project Baker*."

Rumbling, Shepherd narrowed his eyes. "You should not go through my COM."

"Is that really what date night was called?" Cackling from the look on his face, tears came to Claire's eyes. "I was joking!"

Handing him a large glass filled with the most unappetizing shade of green Claire might imagine, she said, "Bottoms up. We are expected within the hour."

Because it needed to be said, Claire explained to the man chugging down a meal that no blend of fruit or herbs might ever make palatable, "And to be clear, I am not talking to anyone but you."

∽

ONE STIFF HAND hosted a chilled coupe sparkling with a pink drink. Claire's other palm gripped tightly to Shepherd's hand, their fingers interlaced. Sweating profusely, she hid her body behind her mate's mass and peered around him to soak up the quaint cobblestone courtyard.

Pruned shrubbery outlined the formal shape of the space. Wrought iron tables displayed an array of snacks. Cushioned chairs had been prepared for relaxing.

Candles flickered, casting soft light that warmed the evening air.

Not that the courtyard needed warmth. Greth Dome was downright balmy, sticky hot with the season as if the sweltering temperatures of the jungle seeped in—just as snow had once seeped into Thólos.

Yet it was always darker in this new place.

Endless fields of glittering white had made the sun shine so bright in Thólos' eternal winter. Sometimes… it had been blinding.

Greth was softer on the eyes, despite the bright colors favored by its people.

"Little one, where would you like to sit?"

Speechless, aware of the irony, considering it had been

her decision to contact Dr. Osin and order the event. Claire didn't even know where to begin.

Her husband had planned this down to the last twinkling bulb. She could never pretend it was not extremely pretty and very sweet.

"I think I'd like to stand." Claire took a sip of the drink in her hand. Pulling back from the coup with a look. "This has alcohol."

"It's a local drink, *a Caipirinha*, with muddled strawberries."

Tongue tracing a bottom lip sweetened by sugar, Claire admitted, "I can't even remember the last time I had a cocktail in public."

All male, grumbly with the pleasure of seeing his female enjoy herself, her husband swelled with pride. So much so, he might actually have burst out of his shirt.

Teasing, she held the drink up in offer. "Want to try it?"

"Yes." Shepherd fell upon her, taking her lips to suck them clean and then delving deeper to capture every last trace of sugar.

He kissed her as if he didn't care who might see or how vulnerable they might be when distracted. And then he kissed her some more.

Bending her back with the heat of his kiss, he drank deep —filled her with breath when she gasped for air, and invaded her mouth with his tongue.

Claire… had never been kissed in public. Modest and blushing when he pulled back to take the drink from her hands and swallow.

Suddenly shy, she glanced at the party of strangers to see who might be watching. "I feel like I'm being courted."

"Hmm." The man who had woken in her perfect nest and drank his gross dinner grinned.

Shepherd grinned.

"Stop that! You're making me nervous."

"I love you, little one."

Rubbing at her breastbone, Claire offered a very distracted reply, "Yeah, yeah, I love you too. But please stop that. It's not safe."

Because if she dripped slick, terrible things would follow. An Omega could never, *ever*, be aroused in public. She had not committed to this to inspire a bloodbath.

"Claire."

She'd heard him speak, but she was still checking every corner, praying nothing might drip from her vagina to scent the gusset of her panties.

"Claire," Shepherd called to her with more force. "Take a deep breath."

She did on command, not that she would do anything else.

"You are safe."

Panting, already pulling away, she said, "I think we should leave."

"Take another deep breath."

Was he out of his mind? They were outside. In a courtyard. All courtyards in Thólos had been brimming with decomposing corpses. Bodies would have been swinging from the pretty trees. "Will you *please* stop!"

"One more breath. Hold it and count to six."

Tears were running down her face, Claire not even sure why. "Gods, Shepherd. We have to go home—"

"Please don't be afraid. The other women here will look to you, and they are frightened too."

Unable to bring herself to glance beyond the hands pressed to her face, Claire sobbed.

How had she become this pathetic woman? This frightened rabbit who jumped every time a glass clinked or soft laughter filled the air?

What happened to the woman who had trimmed her hair, who had styled it similar to a fashion she had seen on her COMscreen?

What happened to the fierce mother of Collin who had survived Thólos?

"You're doing well, little one."

Embraced in the massive arms of her mate, she ruined the front of his pressed shirt. Not that he would ever care. Shepherd just purred for her. He gave her time.

When the panic began to pass, she pulled away, embarrassed and certain she would never leave her house again.

But a smiling older Omega pressed a fresh drink to her hand, kissing her on both cheeks in a style Claire had only seen in the programs on her COM.

And Shepherd had let her.

Hand shaking so hard the ice hit the side of the glass, Claire took a sip.

It did taste like strawberries.

And sugar.

Lime.

And a sort of liquor that had never slipped over her tongue before.

Huge thumbs swiped over pink cheeks, Shepherd praising her bravery and unabashed about how loudly he did so.

The shift was not immediate, but it was measurable.

Feeling came back to her fingers, then her legs. Thankfully, her dress left her arms and back bare, her sweat hardly making a mark.

Staring up at a man who could exercise remarkable kindness, Claire whispered, "You need a haircut."

And they laughed.

Because he had seen the tufts of black hair she had left all over their bathroom floor.

Slate gray, iron gray, the gray of a freshly polished silver, the most beautiful eyes she had ever seen—he who stood amongst the social gathering, dressed like a *regular man*, asked, "Are you ready?"

Heart pounding so hard it hurt, Claire swallowed down another sip of sweetness, quoting Sun Tzu, "*Can you imagine what I would do if I could do all I can?*"

"Yes, Claire." Stroking his hand down her spine as he turned her toward the sparkling courtyard, he said, "That is why I fear you above all others."

"You're not funny."

"You think I am funny."

Smirking, she took another step over cobblestones and moved nearer where other couples were engaged in their own conversations. Then it sank bone-deep. Shepherd won every war he'd ever waged.

Thólos fell. It ate itself just like he'd wanted it to. Greth now belonged to him.

What would he have done to this place if he had found no Omega mate in Thólos?

What would he have done to the world had they never met?

If Svana had...

He certainly would not have filled courtyards with happy people and the sweet smell of freshly baked things. There wouldn't be pink drinks. The man didn't care if the air were chilled or balmy, if the music were vibrant or morose. He would never care for the taste of good food unless she held up her fork and offered him a bite from her plate.

Shepherd craved only her.

Moreover, the villain would never deny it.

Patient, utterly still, Shepherd allowed Claire to stare at him in full understanding, purring as if he knew she finally realized her place in the world. Yet the almost unbearable weight of his silver eyes said, *"You love me, and there is no undoing it. I love you so fiercely you will never be free of me."*

"Shepherd..." Swallowing, her mouth suddenly dry, Claire tried to find the words. "The responsibility of containing you is more than I can handle right now."

Unmoved, he offered a simple smile.

Where other breathing humans could see.

Gulping at her drink, Claire gawked at him over her glass.

"The woman in the striped dress," Shepherd began. "Her name is Regina. The man speaking to her is Phillipe. After his arrest five years ago, she was locked in a brothel frequented by powerful men. When Thólos fell, he climbed free of the Undercroft, found her, and then went on a rampage to kill every man whose name was on the books for having *rented* his mate."

Green eyes observed the distant couple, who spoke with smiles, sipping their drinks. They looked *happy*.

He looked every bit the jaded, scarred, and marked Follower. A killer. Yet it seemed it was she who offered comfort by leading the interaction, by gently touching his arm.

As if being here was difficult for him and necessary for her. Like Shepherd, he didn't want his mate out of his immediate eye line, but wanted to give her this.

A simple movie with others. An opportunity for... normal.

For a woman who had suffered what Claire had only known for one *horrendous* day.

Nearer a planter blooming with red poppies and vaulted by a pretty fruit tree, a reticent female stared anywhere but at the decidedly unattractive face of the Alpha at her side.

Claire asked, "Who is that?"

"Guadalupe. Newly mated and frightened." Shepherd put an arm around Claire so they might observe together. "I have known him for twenty years. You will not find a better man."

That remained to be seen.

As if he could read her thoughts, Shepherd added, "Peter is madly in love. Has been from the first time he saw her in the market. He courted, offered, and won."

"Won?"

"Her bond." Said with such innocence it was clearly pure bullshit.

Warning him with a tone that brooked no refusal, she growled, "Shepherd…."

"Ask her yourself if you desire the details."

Now, he was starting to piss her off. "I can smell her fear from here."

"She can smell yours as well."

The nest she had built for him, she was going to rip it apart herself once they got home. "You think it's funny to parade rape in front of me?"

"I think you should get to know Peter before you judge him by his face." After audibly cracking his neck, Shepherd added, "And if you are feeling magnanimous, you should get to know Guadalupe as well."

There was no reason to keep her voice down. "You are trying to pin the problems of your inept Followers on me!"

Shepherd, patient and gentle, cuddled her closer. "I am trying to entice you to teach me what is to be done when watching a film. I have never seen one in a public setting before."

Instant guilt, laced with extreme suspicion. "Honey, if you want a *normal* experience, don't title the mission *Project Baker*."

"Noted."

"I can't help your Followers," she added, just to make sure he understood that she was going to return home when this was done and burrow.

"Guadalupe has studied horticulture her whole life. She is coming to plan the new layout for the orange trees I have prepared for your garden."

"You're an asshole."

"Shush. The movie is starting."

22

BERNARD DOME

Fingertips to the windowsill, Brenya explored the red-stained wood. There were pock marks from age, telltale signs of who had lived in such a strange room before. Notches where there had been frustration or force or even accidental brushes with something that indented the wood forever. New marks she could account for.

"You are to escort me to Beta Sector today, Brenya. I would like a tour and full accounting of Palo Corps."

Nodding, her eyes still on the view, Brenya replied, "Yes, Commodore."

As if he had not been tripping her up with weeks' worth of difficult scenarios, Jules Havel called from where he worked. "There is an update on the state of Annette. She has transitioned out of quarantine with her son and taken a residence. She has been tasked with educating the population on the culture of Bernard Dome."

"An Ambassador?" They were giving her friend an important position? Strange warmth moved through Brenya's chest at the idea of Annette hosting tea to new people. "She will be an excellent Ambassador."

Jules added further information. "George is still suffering withdrawal. There is no further update on his status."

There was no jealousy in his voice when it came to the name George. No ripple in the emptiness inside the Beta.

Brenya had no idea what to make of this new Commodore. Found herself frustrated more with his distance than his demands.

Turning to look at the man who chose to work from bed most mornings, using her hair as a shield as if he would not notice her attention, she found the sight growing familiar. Pillows at his back, an unusual COMscreen propped on his lap, he lounged, focused on his work.

Very little that he did made sense.

From that first night in this bed.

The clinical way he had observed and tended her naked flesh. The questions, the strange manipulations down her spine. That he had ordered her to bed, and when she had obeyed, a man who had promised her that Bernard Dome would know no mercy pulled the covers up under her chin and told her in a softer voice to sleep.

After slipping off his coat, he had joined her—trousers on, shirt on—and made no move to touch her as she stared at the carved wooden canopy above.

The cool sheets felt so different from the soppy mess she

had left when Lucia had yanked her from her bed. They were smooth, even stiff. A bit musty even.

Red Consumption in Bernard Dome. A Red Room to sleep in. Ancil's red blood still on the floor.

The man shifted, turning to his side to stare at her as the sun began to rise, yet still, in no places did their bodies touch.

Adrenalin fading, she shivered, even her teeth began to chatter.

Annette, her baby, and George were in the air on their way to a new home. Ancil was dead. The very Beta she had wronged and tried to save only hours ago was lying next to her naked body, staring....

All her focus had been spent on one task, and it had been achieved. It felt like her sorry grip was beginning to slip, and Brenya was about to fall down the side of the Dome again.

The hiccup came first, surprised her so much her hand flew up to cover her mouth. And then another, and another, until she was heaving from the effort of holding back.

The ugliest of cries broke free, one that had been growing inside her from the day Jacques Bernard had torn her in half. Brenya didn't even understand when she had sat up to brace her elbows on bent knees, to hold her skull in place as the mess inside came out.

"Are you familiar with the concept of shock?"

Yes, she was. It was a common response to physical trauma. Yet even when she had fallen from the Dome, it had not manifested with so much noise.

The man moved a pillow, tucking it to her side. Then another, all the while saying, "I was given a report on your behaviors, yet thought it would be best to observe them for myself before concurring with an outside perspective and a dossier I had less than ten minutes to read. It is obvious that you have not been guided on how to be an Omega. Your dynamic was manipulated instead by a boy who lacks control and experience."

Another pillow, the very one he had been sleeping on, was added to the pile that grew around her and between them.

"You do not understand the difference between a nest and a bed, nor were proper nesting materials made available to you." The blanket was doubled over, Jules left with none, once it was folded over the circle of pillows. "It never occurred to you to ask me for them tonight."

Slipping back against the softness, teeth chattering and unable to breathe through her nose, Brenya sank into the strange cocoon as if it might actually keep the Beta male away from her.

It didn't even matter that the pressure against her stitches was uncomfortable and that everything smelled musty and unused.

The mattress shifted in such a way she knew, even buried under the bedding and unable to see, that he had moved away.

The offer was as stony as every other word she had ever heard the man speak. "Considering that I am your husband, it is appropriate for me to offer a purr."

"No." Purrs were unsettling in their ability to make

mental switches short. Enough synapses were firing in her brain.

"Sleep. We can talk more after you have had a chance to rest and collect yourself."

He didn't seem like the sort of man who talked, but so long as he continued not to touch her, she would agree.

Sleep did come. It seemed like it never would, but it did.

Groggy and stiff, she woke to a bladder near bursting—still contained in the pillow construction.

The sun was in the exact same place in the morning sky it had been when she shut her eyes. But the Beta had moved from the bed. Lashes crusted, Brenya rubbed the sand away, blinking to see him making use of one of the many available plush chairs, working. Flipping through whatever data filled his COMscreen.

Without looking up, he acknowledged that he knew she was both awake and in need. "The bathroom is behind the panel to your right."

Unsure how to slip from the bed without disturbing the circle of pillows, Brenya crept over them, toe pointed to find the floor.

The Beta did not look up.

"Clothing is on the counter. When you return, there is a pitcher of water waiting by the table with flowers. It will help with your headache. You're not hungry, but you should eat as well."

Jacques had never talked to her this way, in suggestions that did not linger with threat should she decide to refuse them.

Panel was literal, and not in a maintenance sense. One of the red-stained, shining portions of the wall had parted open like a door. It was a door, on hidden hinges that clicked shut when she tested it. And clicked again with a firmer push.

Swinging open, it displayed a bathing area. There was no sunken tub like the one in Jacques' rooms. This one was above a tiled floor and had clawed feet like those of a gryphon. The windows were high atop the walls, small, and made from colored glass. The sun cast light like a prison over a large mirror surrounded in golden depictions of the Gods in their cherubic forms. That mirror, in turn, cast the light back to the opposite wall.

Calculating the angle of refraction was quick and comfortable. Marveling at the hidden details all over the room so distracting she almost forgot her body's needs.

First, the toilet, then a shower... both moments done without any interruption. Not that Brenya did not watch the strange door, waiting for the Beta to intrude.

But he didn't.

And as he said, there were clothes. Loose-fitting trousers that cinched with a simple string at her belly, and a shirt. Jules' shirt from the smell of it.

Nothing chafed, though it was breezy and unfamiliar. Most of her was modestly covered aside from where the shirt parted at her throat.

She used his comb.

Brushed her teeth with the second, waiting toothbrush.

When all was done, she studied her cheek in the mirror. The yellow of iodine had faded between sleep and bathing, the skin pink and outlined on one side by a reddened scar and the other by ordinary bruises.

The patch on her neck had been removed before bathing, and Lucia had been right. With the abscess drained, there was finally a normal scab.

And every morning, it looked a little better.

He never touched her, though they shared space many hours of the day. The closest he came was his day-old shirt on her back each morning, and the bed they shared each night.

Though even that had become something that no longer looked like any bed she'd ever seen. It started with little additions he'd placed here or there. More blankets, extra pillows in a variety of colors beyond the red of the room.

Nothing was white.

The man only wore black. No embellishment, no embroidery, a stark opposite of what Brenya had seen in Central. Imagining him standing before Parliament in such pristine starkness, it was easy to see that the other men would look even more foolish beside the Beta who had taken power.

Brenya never left the room.

The first time he had, she had followed procedure upon his return. Arms around his neck after he entered, she'd asked which chair he might find most comfortable. When she had reached for the fastenings of his trousers, though he was obviously hard, he had taken her wrists and pulled her hands away.

He did not look pleased as he demanded, "What are you doing?"

What was she doing? Embarrassed and oddly *insulted*, she had given no answer. After all, she had clearly asked him that first night not to use her mouth while she had stitches... and he had not.

Throwing off her touch, the Beta walked away. "Go for a walk."

"I'm sorry. A walk?"

"Leave the room, Brenya. Walk anywhere you want. You have your own guards waiting to escort you."

"Anywhere I want?" It was a trick. It had to be a trick. The one and only walk she had taken since coming to Central had almost started a riot.

It was like he could read her mind. "Standard protocols have been put in place to move unmasked male populations away from areas Omegas want to stroll from noon until four. As you are my wife, and as I trust you not to abuse your people's schedules, I expect that you will do your best not to inconvenience those who are working should you wish to leave the grounds at other hours." Back to her, his voice barked a stiff, "Areas can be suggested for you to tour. No one will touch or bother you."

She did not want to go.

Life had been somewhat palatable in the Red Room. The food had been simple, the hours had been quiet, and there had been no buzzing pliarator or bruising grip.

"Get out!"

Her skin might have been left behind she ran so fast. Throwing open the door, dressed only in his shirt and another pair of plain drawstring pants, she found the guards—biosuits, armed, reliant on canistered air—waiting.

"Greetings, Mrs. Havel."

Before she might untie her tongue and form some kind of reply, a shot of pleasure spiked right between her legs. On a gasp, she put her weight against the door at her back and felt an uncorked wave of slick go right down her leg.

Lightning struck her spine, a tiny pool growing at her feet as electricity spread from leaking, empty cunt to every extremity.

Seconds away from blinding orgasm, fighting the urge to reach into her pants and ferociously rub her throbbing clitoris, Brenya pointed at a door across the hall. "What is in there?"

"Every room in this quadrant of the Palace is vacant."

Perfect. She ran the short distance, throwing the door closed and locking it before any of the men might see her fall to her knees. The scream of her climax was trapped, Brenya having bit down on her forearm until she tasted blood.

Dazed when it was over, finding herself sprawled on hands and knees—fully presenting—she rolled to her back and panted at the ceiling.

Projections of this very fresco were available in the museums. The story of the Red Consumption and the lovers torn apart. Cloaked Death pulled naked women from their reaching men. Women from women. Men from men. No love had been spared.

Famous poets summed up this work, long dead yet still remembered.

And it was right here, in a vacant room where all the furnishings were draped to protect from dust and light.

Aftershocks still quivered between her thighs, her confusion blending with relief... and also humiliation. She knew she should not have left that room.

One look at Alpha guards and this is what became of her?

No wonder Jacques thought she enjoyed his attention.

A light knock came to the door. "Madame, the Commodore has suggested you return to your room and rest. He says you will not be disturbed for the remainder of the day."

Why she laughed, Brenya didn't know.

Jules was gone by the time she found the energy to peel her body from the soaked floor. Padding barefoot across the hall, she went right back to her home in the Red Room.

Bernard Dome's new Commodore returned at dark, stern as he asked her to take a seat across from him.

Glaring.

The very look of Jules Havel was so intriguing that she stared right back.

Tension did not exist between them, even though it was neigh an hour before he broke the silence. "Whatever *training* you received from Jacques Bernard is not a performance I expect from you."

"What do you expect me to perform?" So far, the only thing he had ordered her to do was walk, and that had not gone well.

"The Queen of Greth Dome has asked my permission to exchange letters with you. She is a kind woman and someone

I respect. The first arrived today, along with pictures of a painting she is creating as a gift. I believe it would be appropriate for you to create a gift in return."

Sweat prickled Brenya's brow at his tone, Brenya's thoughts darting to the slick-soaked pants she had stuffed into a crevice in the bathroom.

Without missing a beat, Jules Havel continued, "You have a skill for clockwork, I understand. You dropped a cog in my ship."

It was she who broke their extended eye contact, glancing to the side while scenarios flipped through her conscious. Make a clock? From random pieces? Not just take one apart and put it back together. "Yes, I would very much like to make the Queen of Greth Dome a clock."

Very much!

Little tools and gears. Hours focused on the minutia. There would be so many glorious mistakes.

Twitching fingers were already working imaginary bits and bobs. Ships were relatively big. It could be as tall as Jules. No! A small clock would be more difficult to calibrate. More fun!

"Then it is settled. Everything you need to sketch out schematics will be waiting for you in the room across the hall. That will be your workspace. The fabrication department will queue your request behind daily necessities and emergency work."

"Can I start now?"

"No." A male who had glared so ferociously the moment before almost smirked. "I find myself at a place in life where

I understand the need for balance between work and *pleasure*." Jules said that last word as if he didn't fully understand it.

Pleasure? Clearly, he was ready for her to perform, Brenya already sliding to her knees to *pleasure* the man as she had been taught.

Shooting to his feet, Jules roared, "Get up and sit back in your chair!"

None of it had been intentional, yet she had ruined her chance to make a clock. Sadness crashed, the wave breaking apart the brittle excitement she'd known.

"Hear me, woman!" Grabbing the glittering vase of flowers that came each day when the breakfast cart was outside the door, Jules Havel threw it to smash into a cascading shower of glittering crystal. The window he had aimed for solid as it had ever been. "You are not permitted to touch me unless you want to!"

Her eyes stung, but she refused to ruin this further by crying... or speaking. Rapid nods were offered instead.

The man actually ran his fingers through his hair, mussing the short ends in a very human gesture. "It's not your fault."

"Sometimes, I see things inside you that suggest something I felt constantly from Jacques. You don't touch me, but you want to. *I want to build a clock.*"

"Do you want me to touch you?"

He knew the answer was no. The question had been a reminder that she slept deeper and deeper inside her circle of pillows.

From anger to hunger to longing, brief flashes of emotion each differing in their taste, and each fleeting. Vanishing from Jules Havel's mind as if they had never existed.

Their stare began again, only this time, the man seasoned it with words that she would never forget. "When you are ready, you will come to me, and though I promised once to hurt you, you have my word that I will not."

Again, she was the one who broke their gaze, looking to the mess for something to do besides sit and grow warm.

When she moved to stand, he lifted a hand. "Don't touch the glass. Your mind and body have enough to heal as it is."

Three Alphas armed with a vacuum, floor wax, and a tray of simple food came and went in a blink.

Brenya ate gruel, smiling at the taste. The man drank something that stank of rotting tubing. And then they went to the separate ends of their bed.

In the dark, Brenya could have sworn Jacques touched her hair, shrieking as she roused from sleep to scrabble away before he might mount her.

The nest of pillows scattered, Brenya locking herself in the bathroom as if that trick might work.

She'd seen the man rip the door from his own lavatory. That didn't stop her from bracing against the wood.

Jules' voice came instead. "When you are ready to come out, there are matters we need to discuss."

He did not sound angry. Glancing into the emptiness of him, the Beta was the same neutral calm as always. But Jacques, Jacques was scratching for attention just enough to bring gooseflesh on her body.

Minutes passed, and she felt more foolish. Jacques Bernard was not in the room. He hadn't been any of the times she had jumped at shadows or thought she heard his purr.

Unlatching the door, she found the Beta rebuilding her nest. Shy, she went to help him, altering the placement of a few soft things for optimal structural support.

"When an Omega is parted from the person they share a pair-bond with, mental decline commences. Auditory hallucinations, physical reactions, nightmares." The perfunctory way in which Jules said these things, it made it seem immaterial, manageable.

It felt no different than a supervisor outlining her duties for the day.

Handing her the last pillow to place wherever she wanted, he met her eye and took the fresh calm of the moment away. "Jacques Bernard has been under a medically induced coma, a feeding tube ensuring he receives optimal nutrition. However, this situation is unsustainable. It is clear to me that it would be in your best interest to have Jacques *functioning*."

That was why the Alpha's psyche had withdrawn like low tide. He was there, but he was quiet, and the idea of him crashing back in left Brenya shaking her head. "No."

Jules Havel explained further, emotionless and unresponsive to her refusal. "There will be times you will be required to tolerate his presence. How often those moments arrive will depend on your reaction to his absence."

Shaking her head more firmly, she clutched the last pillow to her chest. "No."

"He will be assigned to tend Lucia through her pregnancy."

Brenya didn't know what that meant, and she didn't care. "Please don't give me back to Jacques Bernard!"

It looked like the Beta considered reaching out to touch her, wielding a firm voice instead of a soft touch. "You share a pair-bond with the Alpha. He will be an unavoidable nuisance for the rest of your life. But do not imagine that I would ever let him fuck you. You will never kneel again to take him in your mouth."

When he gestured for her to climb into her nest, she did, retreating under the covers as if the whole night might go away.

Jules underestimated Jacques' obsession if he imagined the Alpha would leave her alone.

A warm purr came from the Beta climbing into his side of the bed. An auditory caress that was so different than the purrs she experienced in the past.

Yet it worked the same; her eyes grew heavy, and the knot in her stomach loosened. A strange hum fell from her lips, Brenya floating on the cusp of sleep.

When the phantom touch came again, she didn't scream.

She slept.

She woke, she dressed, she looked through the information the Queen of Greth Dome had organized for her. The final note was from Jules, informing her where she might find a space set up for her work.

Upon preparing for her day, her heel found a single missed shard of crystal. It burrowed in, cutting her foot as she padded dazed across the floor to the room she had discovered the day before. Tiny droplets of blood were left behind to soak into the wood.

She would not think of Jacques. She would think only of gears and what might be done with them.

Under the fresco, bathed in great light, simple supplies had been prepared for her. A drafting desk, paper, pencils, the tools of the trade for the life she had once lived.

Hours later, Jules pulled the shard from her heel, Brenya ignoring him as her pencil flew over a tilted desk.

Standing over her shoulder, near enough she could feel the heat of him, already saturated in the subtle scent of him, Brenya explained what he had not asked. How this clock would work.

She talked for ages, flipping through the pages she had drafted, her hair wild, her voice alive.

Everything was wonderful, until she felt his lips brush her hair.

The unnamable wave that had followed confused her.

Unsure if she even felt what she thought she had felt, the tickle on her scalp no different than any breeze, Brenya dropped her pencil. The sound it made as it rolled from her tilted desk to the floor was deafening.

"You were saying?"

"This part..." Had she really just called it a *part?* An integral piece of machinery was so much more than so rudimentary a title.

Male arms braced against the desk as he leaned forward

to look. The heat of Jules' body seeped into her as if they actually touched. "Yes?"

"I read the letter from Greth's Queen. She sent me pictures of things I'll need you to explain to me if you want me to understand the context enough to reply."

She refused to lift her eyes from her draft but could *swear* the Beta was smiling. "Such as?"

"Jules… I am—" Brenya swallowed, working to keep her breath even. "—not sure this clock will be an equivalent to her painting."

The man's right hand lifted from the table, the edge of his fingertips running along her throat until they lightly traced the bite mark on her neck.

It was the growing tightness of her nipples that awakened her to the sound she had made. Snapping her head straight, she stood, her back hitting his chest, so she might circle the desk and move an appropriate distance away.

Her first thoughts were so random, so wrong, that she hated almost telling him to file a request for a mental hygiene visit. That after requisitions approved, she would have the formal paperwork stamped and he could have sex with her just as she had done with George.

Her second thoughts were of embarrassment—because, of course, she had imagined the touch. It had been nothing more than another hallucination.

And her third?

Her third was that she wished it had been real. That she wished he would order her to her knees.

"Brenya."

Already growing limber, she leaned closer. "Yes?"

"I cannot join you for dinner tonight."

"Oh." She took a step away, unsure why she kept touching her hair. "Um."

"It's going to be a spectacular clock. Promise me you won't stay up too late working on it."

There was no way she was going to be able to work on it until this strange sensation had passed.

He left her.

Alone, the door barred from her side, her back to the floor and her eyes on the ceiling, Brenya looked upon the beautiful fresco of Red Consumption and let her hands stray where they would.

Left nipple pinched between her fingers, labia glistening as her hand touched a part of her that no longer hurt, she came.

The Gods had seen it all. Even the smile on her face.

On the other side of the door, a man groaned. As if he had been pressed against the wood listening to her touch herself.

As if he had shared her climax.

Gathering herself from the floor, cheeks flushed from more than just release, Brenya reached for the latch, only to shriek when a knock shook the wood before she might open the door.

An Alpha guard spoke through the wood. "Mrs. Havel. There has been an incident regarding Jacques Bernard. We are to return you to the Red Room and follow security procedure level five."

The Red Room was less than ten meters away, but she

had been rushed there as if her workspace across the hall were up in flames. When the door closed, it was barred.

It was an hour before Jules came. So much for their dinner apart. He said nothing as they ate plain fare, watching her.

She still felt strange, like he was waiting for her to acknowledge why it seemed so warm in the room. It wasn't until a gasp left her lips and legs involuntarily parted under the table that Brenya went from cautious to frightened.

A knot was blooming, dumping wretched filth.

Shooting out from her chair, staring down at her lap, she found there was nothing there.

Just a small pool of slick she had not even realized had grown between her legs.

"Jacques is awake and, at my explicit order, currently knotting Lucia," Jules began, watching her as she groaned from another unwelcome sensation. "A pregnant Omega who has lost or has been separated from her mate requires *tending*, or her child will abort. He cannot have you. Lucia has no one. It is the solution that benefits all parties… to a point… and will keep the Alpha distracted until he learns control."

Jacques was coming again, Brenya catching her weight on the back of her chair, eyes rolling into her skull.

Whining as if the shrill noise might bring her relief, Brenya squeezed her thighs shut, hoping it would stop the waves of sensation and the churning gush of slick.

Jules sounded almost sorry. "He is your mate, Brenya. The pair-bond cannot be undone. For your own wellbeing, there will be times you must spend in his presence. Is it not better if he is sexually exhausted beforehand?"

"This is because of what I did today?" How she had touched her own body for relief.

"He did not respond well to your pleasure. Even partially sedated, he killed two of the medical team assigned with monitoring him before he could be restrained." Standing from his chair, Jules Havel circled the table and came to her. "But, Brenya, it is your body, and you can do what you want with it. Jacques must learn this and perhaps find a purpose serving an Omega in need."

A conflicting mess ate her up between climaxes, yet one emotion stood out against all others.

Betrayal.

He *had* touched her over the table. That had been real!

Jules had known Jacques was awake… that all of this would happen as a result.

Those eyes that saw everything, that burned like the heart of the hottest blue flame, held no remorse.

Reaching out a hand, a man who had been very *decent* with her, became anything but. Voice pure hunger, Jules Havel purred, "It's time, Brenya. Invite me into your nest."

Thank you for reading CORRUPTED. Read DEVOURED Now!

ADDISON CAIN

USA TODAY bestselling author and Amazon Top 25 bestselling author, Addison Cain's dark romance and smoldering paranormal suspense will leave you breathless. Obsessed antiheroes, heroines who stand fierce, heart-wrenching forbidden love, and a hint of violence in a kiss awaits.

Visit her website: addisoncain.com

Sign up for her newsletter.

Join Addison Cain's Fan Group.

- amazon.com/Addison-Cain/e/B01E1LKWMY
- bookbub.com/authors/addison-cain
- goodreads.com/AddisonCain
- facebook.com/AddisonlCain

ALSO BY ADDISON CAIN

Don't miss these exciting titles by Addison Cain!

Standalones:

Swallow it Down

Strangeways

The Golden Line

The Alpha's Claim Series:

Born to be Bound

Born To Be Broken

Reborn

Stolen

Corrupted

Devoured

Wren's Song Series:

Branded

Silenced

The Irdesi Empire Series:

Sigil

Sovereign

Que

Cradle of Darkness Series:

Catacombs

Cathedral

The Relic

A Trick of the Light Duet:

A Taste of Shine

A Shot in the Dark

Historical Romance:

Dark Side of the Sun

Horror:

The White Queen

Immaculate